Lost and Found

Also by Valerie Mendes

Girl in the Attic
Coming of Age

Lost and Found

VALERIE MENDES

SIMON AND SCHUSTER

SIMON AND SCHUSTER

First published in Great Britain by Simon & Schuster UK Ltd, 2004
A Viacom company

1 3 5 7 9 10 8 6 4 2

Simon & Schuster UK Ltd
Africa House
64-78 Kingsway
London WC2B 6AH

A CIP catalogue record for this book is available from the British Library

ISBN 0 689 86049 8

Typeset by SX Composing DTP, Rayleigh, Essex
Printed and bound in Great Britain
by Cox & Wyman Ltd, Reading, Berkshire

Acknowledgements

My gratitude and love go to Sam Mendes for his generous financial support and unwavering encouragement without which writing this novel would have been utterly impossible; my editor, Stephen Cole, for his brilliant ear and eye, and for being on the same creative and editorial wavelength; and my agents Patricia White and Rebecca Price at Rogers, Coleridge & White for giving me such good and sound advice.

My gratitude also goes to many friends and colleagues in Oxford, Wolvercote, Wytham, Woodstock, Eastleach Turville, and along the Oxford canal – in particular Mark Davies on *Bill the Lizard* – who have made my research so easy and fruitful.

I should also like to thank Ingrid Selberg, Venetia Gosling and the Simon & Schuster Children's Books publishing team for their speed, professionalism and expertise; our copy editor, Lesley Levene; Margaret Hope and Ian Winstanley for another stunning jacket design; and the many booksellers, librarians and teachers who have greeted my novels with such enthusiasm.

Daniel stood by the side of the hospital bed.

He looked down at her.

At the frail, wizened hand trying to hold the spoon.

At the mouth trying to pull the grey mince onto its tongue.

Into the dark-ringed eyes which said: "I am sorry. I can no longer eat."

He reached towards her.

He took the spoon from her hand, inch by inch, and put it on the tray.

Metal clinked against metal.

A gust of wind punched through the curtains.

Daniel took a breath of it.

Then he said, "Goodbye, Gran," and turned away.

The words filled his mouth and tasted of mince.

Daniel

He jumped off the bus from Oxford and swung briskly down Woodstock's High Street, winding through the Saturday shoppers, looking neither to left nor to right.

I'm on a ridiculous mission. I shan't find anyone suitable. And even if I do barge up to some little old lady, she'll accuse me of harassment and tell me to get lost.

At the gates of Blenheim Palace he bought a ticket and moved through the arch to the breathtaking stretch of lake and trees and sky.

I'll make straight for the shops in that courtyard next to the palace. I might find a tourist there. Someone I can spend half an hour with and never see again. Get this stupid assignment over and done with.

He reached the courtyard. It was empty apart from a heavy mottled basset hound who'd been tied up in a corner and sat with his head dismally slumped on the cobblestones.

He leaned up against one of the stone walls, watching. A young couple darted out of the gift shop and strolled away arm in arm, talking in German. Not much chance there.

He pulled a pencil from his pocket and stuck it behind his

ear like they did in newspaper offices. It was extremely uncomfortable, but at least he felt more interesting. *It might make me look as if I mean business.*

A dumpy elderly woman pushed through the food shop's doors. She wore a floppy cotton dress partly covered by an old pink cardigan. Three shopping bags dangled from her arms. Balancing their handles over her wrists, she untied the dog, who leaped joyfully to lick her face.

The sound of splintering glass cut through the air.

"Barnaby!" the woman shouted. "You *stupid* pooch!" She stamped her foot. "*Now* look what you've made me do!"

Six pots of pink clover honey had crashed through the bottom of one of the raffia baskets. The dog squatted on his haunches, looking up at her adoringly. A flush of colour spread swiftly from the woman's neck to her dampening hair.

"Expensive stuff, that honey. Top-notch Oxfordshire . . . Hell's *teeth*, I knew this was going to be a lousy day."

Every day is lousy. Every morning I wake up and there is the poison dart. Wham! *it goes, into my heart. I spend all day trying to wrench it out.*

Daniel stepped across the courtyard. "Here, let me help." He stared at the glistening puddle of honey, lit by shards of glass.

4

"You can't do much with *that*." The woman stooped to stare at the globby mess, as if trying to see her reflection, and poked her finger tentatively into it.

He looked down at her head, at the pile of grey hair shoved into a lopsided doughnut. "I'll get someone to clean it up." He hesitated, reluctant to commit himself. "And then I could help carry the rest of your shopping home."

"You could?" She seemed to register his existence, sucked at a sticky finger.

"That is, if you want to buy some more honey."

She squinted at him sideways, appraising him. "I do. I eat it straight from the jar."

"So do I."

"It's by far the best way, isn't it? Even if it does make you fat." She ran an eye up and down his body. "Course, you're skinny as they come."

He fought through his embarrassment. "The thing is, our school have organised something for today." He swallowed. "It's a special Saturday."

"Special?"

"Yes." He took a deep breath to make sure his voice didn't wobble. The scent of honey seeped into his throat, making him want to cry. "It's 'Adopt a Granny Day'."

The woman gave a snort of laughter. "You mean you're

trying to adopt *me?*" Her flush deepened. "What a bloody nerve!"

"I'm sorry." He looked at the tiny lines creeping around her eyes. The July sunlight seemed to magnify the wrinkles which crisscrossed into a spider's web. "I didn't mean to offend you."

"I might *look* eighty but I'm only fifty-five." Her mouth twitched. "You can't march up to people and make vile assumptions about their age. Who *do* you think you are?"

The energy began to seep out of Daniel's hands. They pricked with pins and needles. They'd done that a lot since . . .

"That's exactly what I said at school."

"*What* did you say?" Sweat trickled down the sides of her cheeks, hung there as if trying to decide where to go.

"That I thought it was a lousy idea." Daniel's voice rushed out louder than he expected. "But Hugo Dodds got up in class and said he thought it would work and that he knew a lot of old people who needed a hand. Mr Anderson, he said it was a wonderful idea, so kind and thoughtful and all that crap." His voice choked. "Look, why don't we forget the whole thing?"

"Why don't we?" The woman tugged at the dog's lead. "Leave that mess there. It'd serve somebody right if they trod in it."

"It would, wouldn't it?" Daniel imagined Hugo Dodds up to his ankles in the sticky white sludge, getting one of his shoes stuck, hopping around on the other leg. Suddenly he wanted to laugh. The pins and needles softened.

"My real gran," he said, "she was my only family . . . She died two months ago."

He looked into the woman's eyes, a speckled grey, bright, attentive, like a bird's. He heard the soft intake of her breath.

"It was the first of May. I got up at dawn to cycle into Oxford, to listen to the Magdalen choir, join in the celebrations. Gran loved doing that. She made me promise I'd go and tell her about it. Later, I went to see her in hospital. It was five o'clock. When I said goodbye, she was still alive. When I looked back from the door she . . ."

"I'm sorry to hear that." The woman shoved at her hair with sticky fingers. "Oh, go on then. There's a first time for everything. Adopt me. Let's give it a whirl."

"*Thank* you." Relief swept through him. *At least I'll have something to report in class.* He slid his notebook from his pocket, cleared his throat in a professional way. "Right. Would you mind giving me your name?"

"Now look here." She bit her lip. "If you put me down as Granny Watkins, I'm off, and so is this stupid pooch of mine. We come as a package, and what's more there's another member of this distinguished entourage back at my place. My cat."

The dog gave a dirty-sounding whine.

"I see."

"That's *right*." She threw back her head. Her hair, which had been threatening to escape the doughnut, slithered down her back. "I'm Laura. He's Barnaby. And madam back home, her name's Muffin."

The dog howled.

"Shut *up*," Laura shouted. "Muffin exists whether you like it or not, you *stupid* pooch."

She turned to Daniel. Her hair hung all over the place, some grey, some a mustard yellow. For a moment he saw her as a young girl, playing by the river, a dimpled sandy bank rippling behind her.

He removed the pencil from the excruciating groove it had dug into his skull. He could smell the pencil's lead, Laura's hair, the pool of clover honey. For some reason he couldn't fathom, the light in the Blenheim courtyard seemed brighter, clearer, more significant.

He said, "My name's Daniel."

Laura gasped as if she had been shot. "My father was a Daniel. He died last year. He was *my* only family. Still can't get used to it, don't suppose I ever will. It was always him

8

and me." Her mouth crooked in a brave attempt at a smile. "Right then, Daniel the Second . . . Who needs more honey? Let's go home."

"I haven't really got a home," Daniel said. "Not any more."

Outside the courtyard, the Blenheim landscape stretched calmly away, the lake smooth and glittering. Seagulls swooped languidly down to it, cawing satisfaction.

"I mean, I've got somewhere to live and people to live with, but it's not the same."

"Let's go the longer way. Over the bridge, round by North Lodge. We can watch the ducks. And a pair of swans I particularly like." Laura pushed her hair out of her eyes. "Tell me about it."

"Not much *to* tell. My parents died in a car accident when I was three. I've lived with Gran in Oxford ever since, in Chalfont Road."

"And now?"

"I've moved over the road. Clare and Martin took me in. They were friends of Gran's. I've known them all my life, it's what she wanted. A couple from social services came to talk to us. I'm seventeen, too old to be fostered, so without Clare and Martin I'd be living in a bed and breakfast . . . I suppose I should count my blessings."

"I assume you *like* them, this Clare and Martin?"

"Yeah, sure. They're kind and all that – but it feels weird. I can't settle. I keep thinking it'll only be for a few weeks." His face burned. "I think about Gran a lot, little things remind me. She was a great cook. Everything I've eaten since she died has tasted of grey mush."

Like that ghastly stuff, in hospital, on her plate.

They walked briskly now, Barnaby tugging at his lead. It was easy to talk to Laura. She was still a stranger, so he felt he could tell her anything, what would it matter? But she was listening, too, as they crossed the bridge, took the path towards the Lodge. A clutch of white geese with fastidious yellow beaks stood, silent for a moment, on the grass to watch.

"After the funeral –" he clutched Laura's two remaining shopping bags more tightly, the words spilling out as if he had little time to talk – "I helped to clear the house. Clare and Martin and I, we dumped the furniture into storage, cleaned the carpets, put the house up for sale . . . It was bought inside a month."

"How do you feel about that?"

"Sad. The money's in trust for me until I'm twenty-one and I've got a weekly allowance. But every time I go to the bank, I just want to have my house back with Gran in it."

"It must be hard, living over the road."

"It is. The new family moved in yesterday. It was horrible. I saw the van arrive before I went to school."

Laura pointed to the lake. "Look, the swans. Aren't they glorious?"

The birds glided past, necks curved and sooty black, feathers a deep gleaming grey, beaks tomato red, eyes watchful and aloof.

"Yes." He stared at their dark reflections in the water. "You kind of expect swans to be white, don't you?"

"Things never are what you expect, Daniel. Don't they teach you *anything* in school?"

"Here we are. Chaucer's Lane."

They turned left from the High Street just outside the spread of Blenheim's arch.

"Mine's the tumbledown Cotswold-stone cottage at the end . . ." Laura shoved a key into the battered paint-crumbling door. "Come in. Ignore the mess. I can't be bothered with housework."

He picked his way over a pile of muddy boots and stared into the untidy living room. On a faded sofa sprawled an enormous ginger cat. She peered up at them, stretching her front legs, claws out, gaping her mouth into a wide pink yawn.

"This is Muffin." Laura stroked her nose. "My beloved ancient heap of orange fur."

Barnaby waddled up to them, growling jealously. Muffin snarled.

"Thanks for carrying the bags, Daniel – or what's left of them . . . Have a seat."

He squashed on to the sofa beside a pile of newspapers, three much-thumbed paperback novels, a dirty teacup and a handful of toffee wrappers. He glanced around the room. A basket of logs spilled into the grate. Shabby curtains, half drawn, looped across grubby windows which overlooked an unkempt garden.

He felt suddenly and gloriously at home.

Laura emerged with glasses of lemonade.

"My father was a spick and span kind of man." She gave him a glass. "This place used to be immaculate." She grimaced. "It's frightening how fast things get out of hand."

"How did he—"

"Peacefully in his sleep." Laura collapsed into a chair. "You may have heard of him. Daniel Latimer, famous historian. He wrote six history books, all bestsellers. He was halfway through a new edition of the third one – a history of Europe since the Second World War. Said he felt tired, went to bed early. Never woke up."

The lemonade caught the back of Daniel's throat. "I'm sorry."

"I was his chief researcher. Trundled into Oxford, to the Bodleian Library, every day. Loved it. Always sat in the same seat, had a sandwich lunch at Blackwell's. Came home, cooked supper for Daddy . . . Not the same any more."

"I know how you feel." Wham! *goes the dart. Nothing will ever be the same.*

"His publishers want me to finish the book. Only four more chapters to do. I know exactly what he wanted to say."

"So why don't you?"

Laura flashed him a warning look. "Easier said than done, young man. No Daddy, no energy. No motivation." She gulped the lemonade. "Gets bloody lonely on my own."

"Where did *he* work?"

"Next door. Haven't touched a shred since he died. Come and see."

He followed her into the adjoining study, dominated by an enormous table laden with maps, papers and books. More books lined the walls, tumbled into piles on the floor. The air smelled of dust and old tobacco.

"It's a wonderful room."

Laura looked startled, as if she were seeing it for the first time. "I suppose it is." She picked up a handful of papers, peered at them, hesitated. "Maybe I should pretend Daddy's still here, waiting for my notes on the next chapter."

"Yes." *I've tried pretending Gran is still alive . . . It doesn't work.*

"So," Laura said, "now you've adopted me, what's the form? I mean, what do we have to do?"

"I don't know." Daniel felt embarrassment creeping over him again. "Suppose I'll have to stand up in class next week and tell them how I found you, where you live, all about you."

"*Will* you indeed!" Laura bridled. "Or the little you've managed to find out so far . . ."

"Yes." He held out his hand. Laura's felt warm and damp. "Thanks, Laura. For letting me adopt you. Stupid idea, really. Didn't think I'd pull it off."

"But you did. I've enjoyed it. Sorry I gave you a bit of a hard time. Haven't got any young people in my life. Forget what it's like."

"Goodbye, then—"

"Tell you what," she cut in decisively. "Why don't we stay in touch? Next Saturday. Come to lunch."

Startled, he said, "That's very kind of you—"

"Leg of lamb, salad, treacle tart." She grinned. "I promise it won't taste of grey mush."

After the boy had sprinted down the road, like he was desperate to get away – and who could blame him, poor little sod: I practically bit his head off and it touched my heart the way he stuck to his guns – I shut the front door, slumped against it like a sack of potatoes.

Then I caught sight of myself in that dratted hall mirror, the one I've always hated because the light falls directly onto it in that ruthless fashion, leaving no stone unturned. I thought, cripes almighty, is that me? That slovenly creature with a sweaty face, hair yellow as French mustard creeping down her back, wearing what looks like the oldest cotton frock in the world?

Best not to notice. Nobody cares how I look, so why should I?

I threw my old mackintosh over the mirror, serve it right, and marched into the kitchen to feed the blithering pooch. Bless his floppy ears. Then Muffin stuck her nose into Barnaby's dish – she's not hungry, she only does it to make him furious – and of course all hell broke loose. I made myself a honey sandwich and left them to it. There's nothing they enjoy more than a good fight.

I wandered into Daddy's study. Not that I meant to, it wasn't a planned expedition. I just wanted to eat the sandwich somewhere with a bit of a different view. For a change. A change of scene. So I sat down at Daddy's table and stared at the sea of papers.

Lots with Daddy's handwriting. The daft, lopsided, drunken-spider sprawl that nobody but me can decipher. It shook me up, I can tell you. I've been trying to avoid looking at it for months. I felt a bit queasy, so I swallowed the sandwich as fast as I could and instead of crawling upstairs to sleep – it's the best way of killing time in these endless afternoons – there I was, prodding at bits of paper, wiping away the dust. Then I noticed a pot of Daddy's beeswax polish in his desk. Lovely stuff, smooth as cream, smells a bit like honey.

I cleaned up a fraction of the room, a jigsaw-puzzle piece, and the dirt was positively alarming. I thought, right, get the cleaners in, first thing Monday.

And in the meantime, Daddy's publisher.

He'd written to me only last week. Again. Good letter, ever so polite. Could I give him a ring, he was longing to know how the book was progressing. The sales of the first edition were starting to drop, but they could be spectacular again with new material. Signed himself *Yours ever, Humphrey*.

Never known a Humphrey before. Come to think of it, I've never known another Daniel, besides Daddy, not until the boy turned up today. Nice-looking lad, lovely green eyes, unusual with hair as black as tar.

I dug the letter out from the pile of sludge. Found the fountain pen, filled it with ink. Said I hadn't been at all well, but I was fast on the road to recovery and any day now I promised I'd be in touch and let Humphrey know how the land lay.

God knows what I'm letting myself in for. Without Daddy.

But I'm going to do it, oh, yes, I am. I'll scramble to the postbox right now, so there'll be no excuses, can't change my mind, no going back.

While I was searching for a stamp, I wondered – just for a moment, one of those brief washes across the centre of my mind – how she was, what she might be doing now, what she was talking about, who she was with.

You know.

Her.

As he turned the corner into Chalfont Road, he saw a toddler race out of Gran's house. For a moment the child stood hesitantly by the gate, his thumb in his mouth, his other hand pushing at his dark curls.

A girl of about Daniel's age ran out after him. She was small, with a soft rounded body and short reddish-gold hair cut in spiky layers. Her dress sang with rainbow-coloured stripes.

"Finn?" she shouted. "Finn! *Naughty* boy! I said *don't* go outside! . . . Now, come indoors and let's find you something to play with."

She hoisted the toddler into her arms, kissing his podgy cheek. She trotted back up the path. The child raised his fists, punched the air and gurgled with laughter as he disappeared.

That's my *house! What are they doing there? How will I ever get used to it?*

He ran wildly into Clare and Martin's, slamming the front door.

"Danny?" Clare called. "Is that you? How did you get on?"

He crashed downstairs to the basement kitchen. "I got the

bus to Woodstock. Met someone in Blenheim, helped with her shopping."

He sat at the scrubbed table, ran his hands over the smooth warmth of the wood. He didn't want to talk about Laura: there'd been something special and unexpected about her. Later, he'd tell Clare he'd be out for lunch next Saturday, invent an excuse. Not now.

Swiftly, to change the subject, he said, "They've moved into Gran's."

"About time too. Not good to let a house stand empty." Clare put a plate of sandwiches in front of him. "Ham and tomato, egg and cress. We've eaten. Martin's at a meeting with the new Oxfam committee."

He stared without enthusiasm at the white bread, already curling at the edges. "Who are they, the new people?"

"No idea." Clare glanced at him. "I suppose this is a stupid question, but do you mind terribly about not being there?"

"Doesn't matter much if I do," he said bitterly. "It's not my home any more. The sooner I get used to that the better."

"Martin and I —" Clare's voice trembled — "we want you to feel *this* is your home now. Anything either of us can ever do for you, you only have to ask."

"I know, Clare. Thanks."

A pang of remorse shot through him. *I should feel much*

more grateful than I do. They'd always wanted kids . . . When I moved
in, that first morning, Clare said it was like I was a late answer to a
prayer.

"Right, then," Clare said briskly. "You must introduce
yourself to the newcomers."

She sat opposite him, smoothing her neat grey bun behind
her ears. He looked at her crisply ironed blouse, her
manicured fingernails; at the gleaming pots and pans, the
immaculate frill of white net curtain, the pruned geraniums
on the window ledge. Suddenly he longed for the untidy
slump of Laura's cottage.

He bit into the egg and cress. It tasted of wet chalk.

"Suppose so . . . I'll give them a day or two to settle in."

But he couldn't stop watching Gran's house, listening for
sounds and voices.

Clare and Martin's house was much larger than Gran's,
which only had a first floor with three small bedrooms. Clare
had given him the large attic room on the second floor which
overlooked the road. He still hadn't unpacked his stuff: every
week he promised himself he'd do it next weekend. But when
he started to deal with the books, comics, old school work,
clothes, they brought back memories so painful that he shut
the boxes, kicked them into a corner and left them to rot.

The windows of Gran's house had been thrown open. As he sat at his computer, tapping out the last English essay of the year, he heard the clear tinkling notes of a piano. Someone started to sing in a pure, confident soprano. Nursery rhymes: "Baa, baa, black sheep", "Humpty Dumpty", "Jack and Jill" piped into the evening air. A child's voice joined in. Then the soprano took off on its own:

"Au clair de la lune

Mon ami Pierrot . . ."

He moved to the window to listen. When the singing stopped, he felt lonely without it.

They're in there, in Gran's kitchen, lying in the bath, sorting out their stuff in my bedroom. Shit. I don't want to meet any of them. And I never want to go back.

But he watched again, later, as a taxi pulled up. A man with a suitcase and a lot of sandy hair was greeted at the door by cries of delight.

Impatient with himself for feeling so curious, Daniel yanked the curtains across his window and shot downstairs for tea. He sat watching a boring thriller on TV while Martin smoked his pipe, telling him between puffs in his slow, self-satisfied way what was going to happen two minutes before it did.

*

Fully dressed, Daniel flung himself on his bed and stared into the darkness.

He wanted to remember the inside of Gran's house exactly as he'd known it. Would the new people build a hideous glass conservatory? Knock down a few walls? Dig up Gran's precious roses?

He remembered her stooping so lovingly over them last summer, humming like a bumblebee, her straw hat tipping over her face, her wizened hands snipping at the dead heads.

He stripped off his clothes. Naked and shivering, he curled up in bed, pulling the sheet and blanket over his face. *I wish I wasn't so skinny. I must've lost weight since Gran died. Sometimes it's hard to eat anything at all.*

He wondered which bedroom the rainbow girl was sleeping in – and whether it was his.

He spent Sunday morning trying to think about other things.

He skim-read the papers. He helped Martin put up six wonky shelves in the garage. He peeled some potatoes for Clare, dreading the mush she would undoubtedly make of them.

At midday he grabbed his skateboard and trundled up and down Chalfont Road, showing off. Two years ago, he'd come second in a competition his class had organised at school for being the smoothest, highest and most skilful skateboard jumper.

He grinned, remembering Gran saying, "Don't tell me. Hugo Dodds came first."

"How did you guess? Hugo won on his frontside nosegrind and his indy grab."

"Good grief!" Gran said. "It's sounds like gibberish to me."

They laughed.

Now, nothing stirred from Gran's. He ground to a halt, picked up the skateboard and walked slowly past the house, willing the rainbow girl to come out. Some of the windows were open, but the front door remained obstinately closed.

Then he had an idea.

He parked the skateboard at Clare and Martin's, summoned up his courage, crossed the road, marched up the path and rang the bell.

The man with sandy hair opened the door.

Daniel said, "Hi. I live over the road, at number 22—"

"Morning." The man pulled his checked cotton dressing-gown more securely around him. "Sorry I'm not dressed yet. Bit chaotic back there."

"Of course." Daniel blushed. "I didn't mean to disturb you." He tried to see into the hall, but all he could spot was a grey teddy bear lying on its back. "Would you like us to leave a note for the milkman for you? He comes to Chalfont Road every morning except Sundays, very early, around five o'clock."

"That's kind of you." The man ran a hand through his hair, but only made it worse. "Hold on a sec, I'll ask my wife . . . Do come in . . . Could you close the door, in case young Finn decides to emigrate?"

With a flutter of dressing-gown, the man vanished. Daniel stood with his back against the door. It was weird — a mixture of terrible and wonderful — being inside Gran's house again, but having to stand rooted in the hall.

The house smelled different: of straw and beeswax, and something pungent and meaty cooking. Packing-cases hunched at the bottom of the stairs. He picked up the teddy bear. It had only one eye, which gazed at him anxiously, as if Daniel might decide to pull out the other one.

The man reappeared. "Eve says could you ask for one pint of full-cream milk and one of semi-skimmed every day? . . . We're the Davenports. I'm Robert but everyone calls me Bobby. Eve's really grateful."

Daniel's hand was pumped firmly up and down.

"My name's Daniel." He was disappointed there was no mention of the girl. "Gran and I used to live here. It was her house for more than forty years."

"You're *kidding*." More pumping. "The estate agent told us about her . . . So sorry and all that." Bobby Davenport opened the front door. "We're *delighted* to be here. I work in Brussels – I'm an adviser for a group of European banks – so I spend most of my time abroad, but it's a *charming* little house."

Silently, Daniel gave him the bear.

"Thanks. Sorry I can't ask you in, we've still got so much unpacking."

Daniel lingered reluctantly on the step.

"You must meet my daughter, she's about your age. Another time."

The door clicked firmly behind him.

I was standing at the top of the stairs, but he didn't see me.

I watched him pick up Harriet and I almost laughed out loud. You can tell when people haven't held a toy in their hands for ages. They turn it round and round, as if it might bite. It's like they're suddenly remembering when they were little.

He didn't have an inkling I was there. I was quite glad of that. If I'm honest, I quite like the look of him . . . But no, nothing serious again for me. I've promised myself.

Not ever.

After he'd shut the front door, Dad spotted me at once.

"Jay? Why didn't you come down and introduce yourself?"

"I've been playing with Finn in his room," I said quickly. "I've only just come out."

"Nice-looking lad." Dad looked up at me and grinned. "Just your type."

I don't know about that.

He vanished into the kitchen and I went back to Finn.

It must be weird for the boy, though. Standing in his own house, seeing other people here.

Us.

I like this house. Mum found it on her own. I stayed in Brittany to look after Finn. Dad was stuck in Brussels at some bankers' conference. Mum came to Oxford for her interview. Once it was over, she rushed straight to an estate agent. This was the third house she saw. She rang me on her mobile.

"Jay?" Her voice sounded all thrilled and sparkly. "They've offered me the job . . . Isn't it great? And I've found us a house . . . You'll love it . . . You can have a room of your own again . . . Yes, I've made an offer and it's been accepted . . . I can't wait to tell Bobby."

That's what I like about Mum. Makes up her mind and suddenly it's all happening. That's why we can live here now, like any ordinary family.

Which on the face of it, of course, we are.

But then I keep reminding myself, I'll have to be careful. It was different in France. English people, holiday home perched on the beach, on its own. Nobody ever knew and why should they suspect?

Here I'll have to watch my step, all the time, every minute of the day, whatever I'm doing and whoever I'm with. Lots of net curtains in Chalfont Road. Neighbours who introduce themselves.

Like the boy.

He's been hanging around. Saw him from the window, whiz-kidding on his skateboard. Must have been watching us, wondering who we are. Good-looking, handsome even, all that inky-black hair reminded me of . . .

But those can be the worst, can't they? The most dangerous. Can get any girl they fancy just by flicking their fingers.

So I must be careful. Be prepared.

It's the details that give you away.

Daniel

School the next day and a long afternoon cricket match kept him away from Chalfont Road for most of Monday.

As he cycled back to Clare and Martin's, he thought about the rainbow girl, wondered what kind of a day she'd had. Gran's house told him nothing. The windows were closed, the Davenports' car had vanished from the drive.

On the hall table sat a note:

> *Daniel*
> *Thank you so much. We got our milk this morning. Sweet of you to think of us. It's beginning to feel like home. Hope to meet you soon when we've found our feet.*
> *Eve*

All week he peered at their house from his window: the instant he woke up, the minute he got home. A decorator's van crouched outside the Davenports. New curtains fluttered at the windows. A basket of white geraniums swung from the porch. Sometimes in the early evening he heard the girl singing. But try as he might, he saw nothing of her – and he could think of no further excuse for ringing at her door.

"Hi!" Laura said. "You're nice and early. Come in . . . Barnaby's pleased to see you! Don't chew Daniel's ear off, you stupid, blithering pooch . . . I'm pleased too."

Daniel gazed around the living-room. "Everything looks different."

Laura grinned. "I cheated. Got the cleaners in, to work some of their instant magic. Course, you started it!"

"Did I?"

"After you left I began to sort through some of Daddy's papers. The dust was inches thick. First thing Monday I rang Top Mop and hey presto! Three girls arrived and transformed the place. I can think again, instead of sitting in a crumpled heap."

"Congratulations." Daniel flopped on to the sofa, which he discovered was a rather beautiful soft blue. "It still feels like home."

"That's a very nice thing to say." Laura perched opposite him. "I've cooked a proper lunch for us. It's the first time I've made an effort for months. Makes a change from honey sandwiches . . . Come and talk to me in the kitchen . . . Have you had a good week?"

"Good and bad. We had this big discussion in class about adopting grannies."

"How did it go?"

"It was a laugh. Not everyone had managed it, so I was pretty proud of the fact that I had. Those who didn't have got to write a boring report on someone famous in the past they'd choose to adopt—"

"So you could be writing about someone as glamorous as Marilyn Monroe!"

Daniel grinned at her. "I'm happy with what I've got!"

Laura looked pleased. "And the bad?"

"The new people in Gran's house. It hit me between the eyes."

"Ah . . . That must be tough."

"It's like their being in the house is pushing out my memory of her." He blinked to deaden the sting of tears. "Not that I've seen much of them . . . There's a girl about my age and a toddler."

"And you want to meet the girl?"

Daniel laughed shyly. "How did you guess!"

"Well, ask her out."

"But I haven't had a chance to say two words to her."

Laura opened the oven and extracted a fragrant leg of lamb, brown and sizzling. "So? Ask her to Sunday tea at your house. Take it from there."

Hunger and excitement clawed at Daniel's stomach. "You reckon?"

"Sure. Ask the whole family. Then you can size her up, see if you like her or not."

"Oh, I like her," Daniel said quickly. "She wears rainbow colours and she sings."

Laura laughed. "It's so simple, the way to a man's heart . . . Do you like roast potatoes too?"

"Roast potatoes and me," Daniel said happily, "go together like bread and jam."

He got home and consulted Clare. Then he darted up to his room and wrote:

Dear Davenports
  Clare and Martin and I hope you are settling in. We'd love to meet you and hope you'll come to tea tomorrow afternoon at four o'clock.
  Daniel

Before his courage deserted him, he raced over the road and pushed the note through Gran's front door.

Then he turned back to Clare and Martin's.

And waited.

Jade

I found the note lying on the hall floor.

I thought, *Oh, yeah, I know your little game. There's nothing worse than nosy neighbours. Once they think they're your friends, they can ask you whatever they like. Before you know it, you've told them all kinds of things you wish you never had.*

So I scrunched it up, but then Mum said, "What's that in your hand?"

"Nothing," I said. "Just a note I found." I showed it to her. "There's *no way* I'm going, so don't even try to persuade me."

"You're being ridiculous. We've come back to England as a perfectly normal family –" that made me laugh – "and if we're ever going to settle down and make a proper life here, we need friends and neighbours, just like everyone else."

I went up to my room to sulk.

It's OK for her. It's *easy* for her. She doesn't understand what it's like for me. How careful I have to be, every minute of the day.

She knocked on my door and then came in without my asking her to.

"Jay, if you're not going, I am. I'll take Finn with me and leave you on your own."

"See if I care." I didn't even look at her.

"I'll tell Clare and Martin – and Daniel – that Bobby's in Brussels but otherwise he'd have loved to come – and that you're not well." Her voice went hard. "If that's the way you want things to be, you'll have to pretend to be ill for the rest of your life!"

Click went the door behind her.

I huffed and puffed for a bit but I could see her point.

I felt like a bit of a prat. I mean, it's only the boy from across the street. So I had a shower, washed my hair, got all dolled up in the blue skirt.

I told Mum I'd go over the road and accept the invitation. I knew she was pleased. She gave me an enormous hug.

"All this will get easier," she said. "The better we settle in and the quicker we do it, the fewer questions people will ask . . . You'll see."

Hmm.

I'm not looking forward to this.

I only hope she's right.

At nine o'clock the doorbell chimed.

He opened the door with trembling hands. The girl stood on the step, shimmering with colour.

"Daniel?"

He swallowed. "Hi."

"Hi."

Her eyes were a deep golden brown, swept with darker lashes. Hundreds of pale yellow freckles littered her nose and cheeks, clung to the tops of her bare shoulders. She wore a long inky-blue skirt with a turquoise top.

"Thanks for the invite."

"It's a pleasure."

He wanted suddenly and desperately to touch her skin, to trace his fingers over the pattern of freckles. Words got halfway to his throat and stuck.

"Dad's in Brussels, but Mum and I would love to come. And my little brother, Finn." She grimaced. "He can be a bit of a handful, so lock up the bone china."

She tilted her head and laughed. The sound rose and fell like a song.

"Great." He wanted to say, "Why don't you come in?" but before he could, she gave a little bob and began to dance backwards down the path.

He said desperately, "But I don't even know—"

She spun round, bounced and bobbed, waved from the gate like a giant butterfly.

"Jade," she sang out. "My name's Jade."

"Got a new house," Finn said solemnly, clutching the bear.

Daniel stared back at him, noticing his extraordinary eyes: one a dark swirly blue, the other frog green. They gazed out from beneath the dark curls, giving his face an enchanting lopsided look.

"I know you have, Finn. Do you like it?"

"Yes. Got own room, for me and Harriet."

Jade laughed. "Harriet's his precious bear."

They sat in the garden, while Clare, Martin and Eve Davenport talked indoors.

"We had a house in London, near Primrose Hill, and then we moved to France. To be nearer to Dad. Finn was born there. He'll be three in September. We lived in a cottage in Brittany, on the coast. Finn and I shared a bedroom, so now he thinks it's *very* grand to have his own."

"You're lucky to have him. I always wanted a sister . . .

I remember when I was six, all my friends seemed to have baby brothers and sisters. I was dead jealous."

Jade dipped her head over her tea, rattled the cup back on the terrace table, reached out to Finn. "You're the best little brother in the world, aren't you? Even though you do sometimes keep us up half the night."

Finn looked up at her. "When will my daddy come, Jay?"

Jade stroked his curls. "Next weekend. Not long now." She glanced at Daniel. "Finn's starts at a new playgroup tomorrow, on the Banbury Road."

"Can Harriet come too?" Finn leaned against Jade, pushing the bear into her face.

"Of course. We'll have to sew her other eye back on!"

"What about you?" Daniel asked, longing to know more about her. "Will *you* be going to a new school?"

"I'm not sure." Jade released Finn, bent to pick up the bear. "I've just taken a lot of exams in France. I've had enough of school for a bit."

"I know how you feel!"

"Mum's got a new high-powered job as head of a language school. She's a very experienced teacher. It's the reason we moved here. And because I got very homesick." She hesitated. "I might start something new in January." She blushed. "I've got a good singing voice. I've always wanted proper training. I might audition for a music college if I can find the courage. Meanwhile, someone's got to take Finn to school, look after him in the afternoons. Might as well be me until he's settled down." She twisted to face him, her eyes flickering dark gold in the sun. "I've a lot of catching up to do in Oxford. I don't know any of it yet. We've been so busy sorting out the house, I've hardly had a chance to put my nose outside the door."

Daniel jumped at his cue. "Maybe I could show you round? I know every Oxford nook and cranny."

"That would be great."

"What about tomorrow? School finishes at half past three. Why don't we meet at four? That'll give us a couple of hours before tea."

Jade stood up. She stared across the garden at Finn, who was roaring through the grass, his arms stretched out on either side, circling the air.

"He's pretending to be a helicopter . . . I'd better go and rescue him." Her loose pink shirt fluttered over her thighs. "Where shall I meet you?"

"Can you find Magdalen Bridge?"

"Sure."

"And in the meantime I'll come up with a plan for your first guided tour."

*

Daniel stood on Magdalen Bridge, watching the gentle swirl of river beneath him, the punts with their laughing occupants drifting lazily by.

Jade's late. Maybe she's not coming. Perhaps she's changed her mind. I was too keen. Perhaps she's got lost in Oxford. I should have offered to pick her up . . .

He looked down the High Street. Jade came running towards him, clutching a straw hat.

"Sorry," she puffed. "Dad rang just as I was leaving. I missed the bus."

"Well, you're here now, so catch your breath."

She stood there, panting and smiling.

"We could wander into the centre of Oxford, watch the buskers. There are some great musicians there sometimes, fantastic to listen to . . . Or better still, we could take the double-decker bus and sit on the open top while it takes us round the city. The tour lasts an hour. It'll give you a great idea of the city's shape, where all the colleges are. You can see some of their gardens through the trees."

He took her arm, feeling the warmth of her skin beneath the creamy muslin blouse.

"The tour sounds great."

"Let's do it, then. We'll catch the bus on Broad Street.

There'll be a guide who'll talk non-stop about the history of Oxford, but I think it's best just to look."

The bus swung round Broad Street, turned left and trundled past Wadham College. Daniel ducked his head beneath the heavy leaves of the plane trees lining the road.

"I had a great idea while I was waiting for you . . . That's the Pitt-Rivers Museum, by the way, the beautiful building on the right . . . Finn will love going there when he's a bit older. It's full of fantastic skeletons."

"What's your idea?"

"We've got an end-of-term ball at school on Saturday. I thought maybe you'd like to come with me, meet some of my friends. It'll be a laugh."

Jade shifted slightly away from him. She dipped her head so that her face was half hidden by her hat. "I'm not sure. I mean, it's sweet of you to ask me. But I hardly know you –" she bit her lip – "and I'm not sure whether I'm ready to go out with you – you know, as if we were a couple on a proper date."

"I see." He squashed the feeling of rebuff. "At least you're being honest. I like that."

Jade flushed.

"Look, I'm sorry. I'm taking everything too fast. It's just

that the ball is soon and I thought it would be such a great opportunity. Only happens once a year."

Jade turned to face him. "Yeah . . ." She pointed. "Oh, look, the University Parks. *That's* where they are . . . I must take Finn."

Daniel leaned back on the seat, swung his arm away from her shoulder. He felt as if he'd been put firmly in his place as a useful neighbour, a mere acquaintance.

He thought about being at the dance. Hugo would be bound to take the glamorous Angela. Woody and Gail had been an item for months. Should he ring Polly? She'd probably say yes, but did he really want to stir everything up again?

No. He didn't. He and Polly were over and done with.

He'd just have to go on his own.

I'd asked the boy whether he'd like to have lunch in Woodstock next time. Daddy and I used to go to the little French place on the corner. It's been so long since I was there it doesn't bear thinking about.

He said yes. I spent all week looking forward to it. Not often I get a chance to go out to lunch.

While the girls had been cleaning up the cottage, I went through my wardrobe and chucked most if it away. Not even good enough for charity. The next day I parked the blithering pooch with my next-door neighbour and drove into Oxford to buy some new clothes. Had an ecstatic letter from Humphrey saying we should meet in London, maybe have lunch near his office. I can hardly do that in the oldest cotton frock in history.

Trying on clothes in front of another punishing mirror made me look at my hair again. I walked into the hairdresser's on the chance they might have a free slot. I was lucky. Greeted me with open arms, thought I must have moved house, hadn't seen me for so long. That kind of stuff. Walked out two hours later with my hair a new conker-brown, cut sleek and shoulder-length, feeling ten years younger – and a lot poorer too. Prices have shot up since . . .

Still, it was worth it. Even Barnaby gave me a second glance.

So anyway, the boy turned up, nice and prompt as always, and off we trotted. Told me he'd managed to meet the rainbow girl – Jade, I think he calls her – and taken her on one of those Oxford bus tours that crawl along at no miles an hour, holding up the traffic. And then, silly creature, she'd turned him down. He'd wanted her to go to the ball with him. Sounds like a fairy tale to me, she must be out of her mind. I mean, at her age I'd have given anything in the world to be his date for the evening.

I could see he was thinking about her, all through lunch, so I prodded him into asking her again. When's the ball? I said. Tonight? So there's still time to ask her.

He said he'd only get the push-off treatment again and this time it'd be really humiliating. I said, maybe she's playing hard to get, some girls like to play games. He said, no, she'd been completely straight and honest with him, she had nothing to hide, it was just too soon.

I said, go on, courage, what have you got to lose? Faint heart never won fair lady. Try again. Use the phone in the corner by the coats.

He stood up, all grinning and reluctant. Said it'd feel weird ringing his old number again.

I could hear him muttering into the phone. I drank the last dregs of my coffee and tried not to listen . . .

It was Mum who made me change my mind.

I'd told her about the bus trip around Oxford and she said it was really kind of Daniel. Then we had a long talk about boyfriends, that kind of stuff. I mean, there'd been André in Brittany, but he was more like an older brother. We went around together for three months and he only kissed me once.

Mind you, that was absolutely fine by me.

So I told Mum about Daniel's invitation to the end-of-term ball.

"You mean you turned him *down?*"

"Yes," I said a bit defensively. "I just thought he was suggesting a serious date. I'm not ready for that kind of stuff."

"Lighten up, Jay. It's only a dance. It's not as if you're going to *marry* him. You'll be in Oxford for a long time, you must make friends. Get out a bit. Don't spend all your time looking after Finn."

So I went up to my room and wrote Daniel a note to say I'd changed my mind. Got halfway across the road with it when I thought, *Wait a minute. He's probably asked someone else. He must know tons of girls.*

I went home and tore it up.

Of course, it didn't stop me thinking about it. Or him.

I even washed and ironed my only long dress, in case we met in the street and he asked me again.

By Saturday I'd given up.

I knew I'd blown it and I was kicking myself.

I mean, how long has it been since I danced? It's one of the things I love doing best in the world. Dancing and singing. They've always been my special thing.

And then the phone rang.

Daniel, calling from Woodstock.

Was I sure about not going?

What would I say if he asked me one last time?

Daniel

He stood on Jade's doorstep.

He retied a shoelace, smoothed back his hair, held the flower self-consciously, finger and thumb. Someone was playing a waltz on the piano in a soft, lyrical way. He rang the bell.

The music stopped.

Eve Davenport opened the door. She had hair the same colour as Jade's, only it was longer and sleeker; the same dark-gold eyes. She looked at him absent-mindedly, as if she were still immersed in the music. Then she recognised him and smiled.

"Daniel! Come in . . . Jade'll be down in a minute."

He stepped inside.

"I'm ready!" Jade came running down the stairs, floating in a long cream dress, her eyes shining. "Hi, Daniel."

"Hi," Daniel said. "You look great." He wished Eve wasn't standing in the hall. "I've brought you an orchid." He gave her the delicate pale flower.

"*Thank* you. It's beautiful." She pinned it on.

He caught the scent of her hair, fresh and lemony. It flickered in dark gold spikes onto the nape of her neck.

"Bye, Mum. We won't be late."

Eve nodded at them approvingly. "Have a wonderful evening."

"Martin's going to take us in the car." Daniel smiled at Jade. "I'm really glad you changed your mind," he said.

The heat in the hall rose steadily as the music thumped and the dancers twirled and swung.

"Enough!" Jade's face gleamed with perspiration. "You've danced me off my feet!"

He grinned, flung an arm around her shoulder, drew her towards one of the tables. They squashed on to the uncomfortable plastic chairs.

Jade ran her fingers through her damp hair. "We had dances in our village in Brittany, but they were usually out of doors . . . Nothing as frantic and noisy as this."

"Daniel!" A plump, blond-haired man with a camera pushed his way through the crush. "Introduce me!"

"Mr Anderson, this is Jade Davenport, our new neighbour . . . Jade, this is my form teacher, Mr Anderson. He's also our school librarian, director of drama – and pretty well the brains behind the school!"

"Welcome to pandemonium." The camera aimed its eye at them. "Smile for Reggie now . . . Perfect!" He leaned

48

towards Daniel. "The photos will be on sale in the office on Tuesday. All profits go towards the school appeal . . . Jade, good to meet you. Have a great time."

He turned to go, hesitated, then dipped to Daniel's side. "I wanted to say well done for getting through the summer term. I know it's not been easy. We're all incredibly proud of you." He vanished into the throng.

"He seems nice," Jade said.

"He is." Daniel swallowed. "He was great when—" Hot tears suddenly filled his eyes. "I'll get us a drink. Don't go away."

"I'm not going anywhere," Jade said.

The dance was magic.

The whole thing, from the moment I put the phone down, thrilled and excited, as if it was the first date I'd ever had. I'd forgotten what that feeling was like: the only thing that matters in the whole wide world is getting ready to look gorgeous for someone you fancy.

Mum saw me skipping along the hall.

"Who was that on the phone?"

"Guess who and guess where I'm going tonight!"

Mum laughed. "So he wouldn't take no for an answer! . . . You're very lucky he asked you again . . . What are you going to wear?"

"The pale green with the short sleeves?"

"Oh, come on, you can do better than that . . . Why don't we leave Finn with Dad and try to find something half decent in Oxford?"

We were lucky. We found an amazing dress, ankle-length, creamy white, with a low back and a lovely gathered waist. We even found some matching shoes.

I spent the rest of the afternoon in the bath, pampering

myself. Mum said I deserved it. Said she was proud of the way I'd coped recently, what with the move and looking after Finn.

She's terrific, my mum. I'm lucky to have her, I know that. There aren't many who'd have been so understanding when, you know, all that stuff happened . . .

And the dance was ace. Daniel's got loads of friends and he introduced me to all of them. I know he was proud to have me by his side.

When he walked me home, he told me all about his gran and what it was like living with her as if she was his mum and dad rolled into one, how much he missed her – how much he'd been dreading someone else living in his house.

I said, on the doorstep, "But are you glad now that it's me?"

"Yes," he said and took me in his arms.

We kissed.

Nothing wild and abandoned.

Gentle, cautious, lingering.

Maybe the first of many.

Who knows?

Promptly on Tuesday morning, he cycled to school and stood in a queue at the school office during the lunch-time break.

But he waited until he was back in his room before he opened the envelope.

He'd ordered and bought three copies of the photo: one for him, one for Jade – and one for someone in Woodstock who was dying to know about the dance.

If it hadn't been for Laura, I'd never have had the bottle to ask Jade again . . .What an evening . . .

He tore at the envelope and stared at the photo.

There they were, him and Jade, sitting squashed together, him with his hair sticking up like a lunatic, Jade all shiny with that dazzling smile, her bare arms curving, graceful as a swan.

He stroked the outline of her cheeks, remembering how they'd walked back to Chalfont Road in the summer evening's light, stood outside Jade's house, touched their lips together in the briefest of goodbyes.

He glanced around his room, at the bleakness of the boxes, the stark wooden shelves. At the pinboard with its drawing pins, holding nothing but bare cork.

Slowly he moved towards it. Into its centre he pinned the photograph.

Well, that's a start, isn't it? . . .

And now for the room . . . If Jade's looking down at me, I shan't feel so alone.

An hour later, grimy with dust, he staggered down to the kitchen with ten empty packing cases. Clare looked up from a letter, peeled off her glasses and smiled.

"Welcome home, Danny," she said.

He dashed across the road.

Jade was wheeling a sleeping Finn up the path.

He called, "Hi! . . . I've got the photo."

Jade turned with her fingers on her lips.

"Sorry!" Daniel whispered.

Jade beckoned. He joined her on the doorstep.

"Do you fancy a drink of something?" she murmured. "We might get a quiet hour before Finn wakes up."

He perched on the sofa in the living-room, staring around him.

Everything felt different: the gleaming oakwood piano against the wall near the window, the scattered sheet music in piles on the floor, the long pale curtains, the new ivory wallpaper, the patterned rugs.

This wasn't Gran's house any more . . .

Jade loved the photo.

"Here." She'd pulled a photo album from the shelf. "Slip it in there."

She'd vanished to the kitchen. He could hear the clink of glasses, Jade singing softly to herself.

He opened the album.

Jade in white shorts and a T-shirt stands on a beach. She looks much younger, her hair long and sleek to her shoulders, her bare feet curling in the sand.

Jade wearing jeans and a sweater, sits in a deckchair, holding a baby in her arms, happiness radiating from her smile.

Dozens of photos of Finn, slowly changing from baby to toddler.

Jade in a group with her parents in Paris, Finn sleeping in her arms.

Jade shopping in a market, bending over fruit and vegetables; standing outside a villa on the beach, Finn tucked into a pushchair beside her; in among a crowd of friends outside a *lycée*, her hair cut short and spiky, her face tanned, her eyes a deep golden brown; sitting at a vast lunch table underneath the vines; standing with a tall blond-haired boy outside a restaurant.

Jade building a sandcastle with Finn, shouting with laughter.

Pushing Finn on the new swing tied to the oak tree at the bottom of Gran's garden . . .

I started to make a real effort with Daddy's study.

Not just the cleaning up — the girls had been pretty thorough — no, I mean rereading the original book, then the stuff he'd written for the new edition, then looking at all the notes that still needed work. I mapped out a schedule I could send Humphrey, so he'd see I was biting the bullet.

I dug out the photo of Daddy. His funny lean face twinkled out at me, sucking on that filthy old pipe. All that silvery hair. Glad he never lost his hair, made him look so distinguished.

My daddy . . .

I propped the photo slap in the middle of the table, so he could keep an eye on me.

Then I went out and tapped on Tim's door. He lives three doors down in Chaucer's Lane. We had a chat over a glass of sherry. I told him I wanted to spend three days a week in the Bodleian and would he dog-sit for Barnaby and I'd pay him? He said he'd love to, it would do wonders for his waistline to walk the dog in Blenheim.

The boy came for lunch. I was so proud of the study that I dragged him straight in there. He said, wow! He could see

I'd made fantastic progress. He gave me the photo of him and Jade at the dance. They both looked radiant. I said I'd frame it and prop it beside Daddy's.

After lunch we went for our usual poddle around Blenheim. The boy said could he take Barnaby's lead? I told him to watch out, that dog's got a lot of pulling power. He said, so what, so did he – look at the way he'd pulled Jade . . .

Seriously, though, the lead's disgusting and rotten and I must replace it.

Barnaby knew Daniel had taken over and nearly dragged the boy into the lake. We had a wonderful walk. I pretty well danced along without having to control the blithering pooch. I told the boy he was making me entirely redundant.

He told me about the dance and the great time they'd had. I said, why didn't he bring Jade to lunch next week, so he could introduce her to Woodstock? He kind of jumped, like it was an idea that had never occurred to him, but he looked all excited, too, so I knew he was pleased.

Then he said it might be hard to prise Jade away from Finn for the whole afternoon. When I asked why, he said he thought there was something a bit weird about their relationship, but he couldn't put his finger on it.

So I said – why don't we ask them both?

Martin looked at him over the top of his breakfast newspaper.

"Now you've broken up, why don't we think about a holiday, just the three of us?"

Daniel hacked the top off his boiled egg. "I'm not sure——"

"We could go to Norfolk and sail on the Broads. Or walk in the Lake District." He glanced at Clare. "Or what about the Edinburgh Festival in late August? There'd be tons of brilliant things to see."

"Can I think about it? I've only just met the Davenports. I'd like to spend some time with them."

"Of course." Martin rustled the paper. "I'm pleased you're getting on . . . We liked Eve Davenport, didn't we, dear?"

Clare, scraping at a slice of burnt toast, agreed.

The week that followed seemed to be full of Jade and Finn.

In the mornings, while Finn was at nursery school, Daniel took Jade around Oxford.

Down to Folly Bridge, where they hired a punt and basked on the river, the water slapping against the banks.

They shopped for fruit and vegetables in the Covered Market, wandered in and out of its dark passageways, soaked in the smells of meat, leather and coffee beans.

They slipped behind the heavy, secretive doors of the colleges — Balliol, Trinity — walked in the tranquil courtyards, sat in the shadows of the old stone walls.

In the afternoons they played with Finn in the garden, swung him in the oak tree, roared around the edges of the lawn playing helicopters. They filled the paddling pool with water, watched Finn gasp at its cool wetness, splash everything in sight.

Daniel helped Jade build a sandpit, digging out a large square of grass, edging it with long planks of wood, lining the earth with plastic sheeting, shovelling the sand into their wheelbarrow, trundling it through the side pathway and into the garden, patting it firmly down.

They bought red and yellow buckets and spades, wrapped them for Finn, watched his delight as he tore open the parcel and ran down to the sandpit.

Daniel got used to carrying Finn. He enjoyed the weight of the child, the way he smelled of Play-Doh and biscuits, the brush of his thick curls against his face. He looked into the one blue eye, the other frog green, trying to answer his endless babble of questions.

"There's a butterfly . . . Why is it white? . . . What are eyes made of? . . . How can I see out of mine? . . . How many ants are there? . . . Why are they in my garden? . . . What do they taste like?"

"Finn asked for you today," Jade said. "When I picked him up from nursery. The first thing he said was, 'Where's Dan?'"

Daniel laughed. He grasped the rough rope handles of the swing, drew them close, pushed Finn high into the air.

The child squealed with delight. "Higher!" he shouted.

Daniel said, "Where else should I be but here?"

Finn clutched Harriet, wildly excited about climbing on a bus.

As it swung towards Woodstock, Daniel pointed out the farmhouses set back from the road, the light aircraft perched at Kidlington Airport, the start of the walls surrounding Blenheim Palace.

Laura took to Jade and Finn at once.

"Come in, come in!" She flung open the door. "So you're the famous Jade . . . Daniel's told me so much about you . . . And this must be Finn." The child smiled shyly up at her and hid behind Jade's skirt. "Come and meet Muffin and Barnaby."

The living-room looked immaculate. Daniel grinned,

imagining how Laura must have hurled everything into drawers and under the sofa before their arrival. But she too looked crisp and smart in a green silk dress, her hair sleek to her shoulders.

Finn, fascinated by Barnaby and Muffin, divided his time between them, pulling at the dog's floppy ears, stroking Muffin's tail while the cat stared at him with slitted, suspicious eyes.

"Jade's adorable," Laura murmured to Daniel as they stood together in the kitchen, putting the finishing touches to lunch.

Daniel blushed.

Afterwards, Barnaby dragged them out to Blenheim. They turned right at the gate, taking the path that dipped to the bridge and the lake.

Finn began to run. He rushed way ahead of them, his arms outstretched, circling the air.

Jade laughed. "Helicopters here we come!"

A plane appeared, high in the afternoon sky. Finn looked up at it, lost his balance, screamed and toppled face forward on to the path.

In an instant Jade had raced towards the child. She knelt on the path and lifted Finn into her arms, stroking his curls, examining his elbows, brushing the gravel from his grazed knees.

Daniel lurched forward to join her – but Laura grabbed his arm.

"No, Daniel, don't go. Leave them on their own for a moment."

"Why? They need my help."

"No, they don't." Laura looked at them oddly, as if she'd never seen them properly before. "I've just realised . . . What a fool I've been! . . . Remember you thought there was something odd about their relationship? Something Jade was holding back?"

"And?"

"It's under our noses, Daniel." Laura turned to look him squarely in the eyes. "Remember the black swans?"

"Yes."

"Nothing is ever what you expect. Right?"

"So?"

"So look at those two, over there. Do you really believe they're big sister and little brother?"

A shiver tingled Daniel's spine. "What do you mean?"

"I mean," Laura said slowly, "I don't think Jade and Finn are brother and sister at all. Finn is Jade's child. He's her son."

Of course, you can imagine. I was kicking myself.

The boy was furious with me, I could tell. He said Jade was way too young to have a child, but he was flailing around. I told him, coldly and deliberately, it was just possible I knew what I was talking about. But then I really wished I hadn't said that.

He told me I was talking rubbish.

His anger made *me* angry. I said, "Why don't you ask her? She'll only prove me right."

We went straight home and stuck plasters on Finn's knees. Daniel wouldn't stay for tea, although I practically begged him. It's the first time he's left without our planning another meeting. I waved to him from the door, but he didn't even look back.

I don't expect he'll bother with me again.

Funny, this stuff about making new friends. It gets harder. As you grow older, you retreat into your shell and sit there, festering. I mean, look at the battle the boy had with me that day we met. I barely gave him a civil word until he started telling me about his gran.

But what I said about Jade, he started it. He told me there was something about their relationship he couldn't explain.

I know I'm right.

The boy probably thinks I'm jealous, that I'm trying to split them up. That's rubbish, of course. I was so happy for him when Jade agreed to go to the dance, and now I've got that photo of the two of them which I look at all the time . . .

I'd ruined the entire afternoon.

We'd had such a wonderful lunch. Finn is gorgeous, with his chubby little arms and legs, those questions he asks, the way he looks at you with those extraordinary eyes, making sense of his world.

I started wondering again about what *she* looked like at that age. So much is happening then, isn't it? The learning of language, how to behave, who loves you.

And who doesn't.

Well, it's too late for me now.

All I can do is wonder what I lost.

I hope to God I haven't done the same with the boy.

Daniel

On the bus, Finn fell instantly asleep in Jade's arms.

Daniel sat with Harriet propped on his lap. He glanced sideways at Jade, filled with mixed feelings: resentment, anger, bewilderment, a peculiar fear — and, despite his heated denial of Laura's suspicions, consuming curiosity.

He wanted to talk to Jade. Properly. Not in a bus full of eavesdroppers. Not with a teddy bear sitting on his lap.

And anyway, he hadn't got a clue how to start.

That night he had a dream full of jumbled images: Finn splashing in the garden pool; Laura standing in the rain, her hair flat, water dripping down her face; Jade smiling up at him as he prodded their punt under Magdalen Bridge; Jade standing with Finn in her arms, the child crying, waving someone goodbye.

Try as he might, Daniel could not see who it was.

He woke with a start, his mouth dry, his body drenched in sweat.

Rain dashed against the window-panes, thundered on the eaves, bounced in rivulets onto the sill.

He heard Laura's voice, echoing through the rain: *"Why don't you ask her? She'll only prove me right."*

On Sunday morning Daniel mooched irritably around the house.

Clare noticed something was wrong. "Are you OK, Danny?"

He shrugged off the question. "Fine, thanks."

After lunch, which he could barely swallow, he grabbed his bike from the garage. Part of him wanted to go into Oxford, into the jostling Sunday crowds, the street-market sellers, the music of the buskers, and to get hopelessly drunk in some dingy pub. Part of him wanted total peace and quiet, to think things out.

Peace and quiet won.

He went for a long cycle ride: down Woodstock Road and round to Wolvercote; past the Trout, heaving with Sunday drinkers, where peacocks shrieked from the trees; into the peace of Wytham village.

He left his bike outside Bridge Farm. Hugo Dodds lived there, but he was the last person Daniel felt like talking to. He struggled up the steep path into Wytham Woods. The university had given Gran a special pass to walk there years ago, and she'd asked whether they would give one to him.

When he'd received it, just before she died, he remembered bursting into tears, knowing that now he'd have to walk there on his own.

The silence of the trees hugged around his shoulders, giving him comfort. Dry twigs snapped like gingerbread beneath his feet. A herd of fallow deer spotted him, turned startled eyes and bounded swiftly out of sight.

I'll have to ask her.

I can't leave things as they are . . . Laura's ruined everything.

I need to know the truth from Jade.

And then what?

How will she feel about me, even if I do find the courage to ask?

He trudged round the semicircle of the woods, back into Wytham. Aching and parched, he cycled slowly home to Clare and Martin's. He climbed up to his room and stared for a long time at the photo of him and Jade . . .

Jade

We'd been mowing the lawn, of all the boring things.

It was a wonderfully cool, clean summer afternoon. Finn was chattering happily to himself in the sandpit. I was wearing my shorts with an old T-shirt and not thinking about anything.

So when Daniel said quietly, "Can I ask you something?" I wasn't listening.

I said, "Of course," but I didn't really *mean* it.

Then he asked me was I sure I wouldn't mind – and suddenly I thought, *Wait a minute, I think this means trouble.*

I'd been cleaning the blades of the lawnmower and I looked up at him.

He was standing there with his arms full of grass cuttings. There was a strange expression on his face, like he was scared or something. I looked him in the eyes and he went all red.

He still hadn't actually *asked* me anything, so I got a bit cross.

"Spit it out, Daniel," I said, "or we'll be stuck here like lemons for the rest of the afternoon."

There was a kind of awkward silence. I remember the fresh scent of cut grass.

And then the words came tumbling out.

"It's something Laura said. On Saturday. She thinks you're not Finn's sister. You're his mum . . . I know it's totally ridiculous . . . But I had to ask."

The garden went all black.

I thought, *So they've guessed! The two of them . . . gossiping behind my back.*

I was hurt and furious and terrified all at the same time, like this huge knot of emotions had gripped my stomach and my throat so I could hardly breathe.

But I made myself fight back. I opened my eyes and forced my spine to stay upright. I clenched my fists to give myself courage and strength.

I hurled myself at Daniel.

I caught him unawares. He dropped the grass.

I pushed him into the flower-bed until he was right up against the wall. Showers of rose petals flung themselves against my face.

I said, "So *that's* why Laura asked Finn and me. To poke and pry into my life."

"It wasn't like that," Daniel gasped.

"Get out of the garden." I spat the words at him. "I never want to see you again."

He said, "I didn't mean anything . . . please, forgive me,

Jade, I'm so sorry . . . I take it all back . . . Pretend I never said a word."

But it was too late. He'd ruined everything.

I screamed, "Get out of my sight."

And then I stood and watched him.

The garden swam up and down in front of my eyes as he stumbled away.

He went up to his room and flung himself on his bed.

His wrists stung. He could still feel her fingers twisting his skin. She'd grabbed him, knocked him sideways with shock. Crushed him up against the wall like she really wanted to hurt him. Thorns on the rose trees – Gran's roses – had seared across his left arm. He stared miserably at the bobbles of dried blood.

All he'd done was *ask*.

There could be only one reason for her fury. What he'd said was the truth. It had to be.

Finn was hers. It made perfect sense.

Except that she didn't want him to know.

Everything was utterly pointless if she didn't want him to know.

"Are you *sure* you're OK, Danny?" Clare blocked his way up the stairs.

"Why d'you ask?"

"You've looked very off colour these past few days . . . And you're hardly eating."

He gripped the banisters. The thought of food made him want to vomit.

"Tell you what, Clare. If Martin's offer of a holiday still stands—"

"I'm sure it does." Relief washed over Clare's face. "Let's go to the Lakes. Some friends of ours have a cottage near Windermere. They're longing to meet you . . . Let's walk our feet off for a week."

"OK."

"I'll ring Martin at Oxfam, dig out our Ordnance Survey maps. We've done some fantastic walks along the fells . . . We could leave tomorrow."

In his room, he shook out a pair of jeans and a T-shirt. They were the ones he'd been wearing when . . . They were still covered in grass.

Furious at the reminder, he threw them into the dirty-washing basket on the landing.

It would serve Jade right if I never came back . . .

In the Windermere cottage one evening, when everyone else was asleep, he tried writing to her.

It was hopeless. Everything was so complicated. How could he possibly put it all into words when he had no idea whether she ever wanted to see him again?

He tore the letter up and flung it into the bin.

He dug a postcard he'd bought that morning out of his backpack. *I know someone who* does *want to hear from me.*

Dear Laura

As you can see from the photo, we're in Windermere. It's great to be out of Oxford for a bit and so far we've only had one rainy day. Martin and Clare and I spend all our time walking. Martin's always a mile ahead of us, Clare keeps up a running commentary on the spectacular views — and I wonder how soon it will be before we can eat our packed lunch!

Hope you're making good progress with the book. Love to Muffin and Barnaby.

Daniel

I knew something odd had happened at Laura's.

It was like she and Daniel had had a row behind my back. Suddenly he was glaring at her, went very quiet, wouldn't look at her. She went all red and puffy. She faffed about finding plasters for Finn, didn't want us to leave, she'd baked a chocolate cake for tea. Made a joke of it. Said she didn't want to sit and eat the whole thing on her own.

But Daniel wasn't having any of it. Just said we had to get back. On the bus going home, he hardly spoke to me. Finn fell asleep and I thought perhaps Daniel was trying not to wake him.

But something had happened. Something serious. I felt it in my bones.

It never occurred to me that Laura would find me out. How long had I known her? How long had she known Finn? Two hours!

When Daniel faced me with it in the garden, I was beside myself. It felt like a conspiracy. I was devastated. I must have been kidding myself pretty hard if I ever thought I could pull it off. I felt such a fool.

How soon now before the whole of Chalfont Road knows the truth? The whole of Oxford? Before Laura starts blabbing to all her friends in Woodstock?

The next morning, Mum and I were having a cup of coffee together after I'd dropped Finn at nursery.

Mum said, "How's Daniel? Are you seeing him this afternoon?"

I said, "No. And please don't mention his name again."

"Have you fallen out?"

"You could say that."

"What's happened? Why are—"

I said bitterly, "Because he and that Laura friend of his have guessed . . . About me and Finn."

Mum said quietly, "I see . . . And you didn't want them to know."

"Of *course* I didn't! Look at the lengths we've gone to to keep it a secret!"

"Sure . . . A secret from the world in general, from people who've got no business knowing."

"You mean I should tell Daniel the truth?"

"If you like him, why *shouldn't* he know? He's hardly going to start blabbing about it to anyone else, is he?"

"Only that Laura woman."

"But they're really close, aren't they? She's like his

surrogate grandmother. They're on your side, darling . . .
And in any case, you should be *proud* to have such a beautiful
child."

"I *am* proud—"

"Well, then . . . What's the harm in Daniel knowing?"

I started to cry. I hugged Mum and I said, "But I threw him
out of the garden and now he'll *never* want to come back."

"Course he will." Mum stroked my hair. "Have you seen
his face when he looks at you?"

I mopped at my tears and smiled at her. "You reckon?"

"Trust me, I'm your mum!"

I calmed down a bit.

I mooched about with Finn.

All week he kept asking where Dan was.

I said, miserably, I didn't know.

Their car wasn't in the drive.

I really *didn't* know where he'd gone – or when he would
be back.

Daniel

He unlocked the front door while Clare and Martin pulled their cases from the car.

Please let there be a note from Jade, a message, anything.

He skimmed through the pile of post. Bills for Martin, letters and cards for Clare, junk mail. Nothing, not a shred of anything, for him. Wait a minute. A card from Laura, inviting him to lunch.

He raced up to his room, plugged the card into the pinboard, peered through his window at Jade's. He couldn't tell whether she was there or not. He turned away, overcome with longing to be in their garden, crouching in the sandpit with Finn, answering his endless babble of questions. Walking in Oxford with Jade's hand in his.

I've ruined everything and I've only myself to blame.

"Back to the grind." Martin squinted at Daniel over his breakfast newspaper. "I must say, I feel better for our holiday. Don't you, Danny?"

"Yes. Thanks, Martin. I meant to say——"

"No need. Good to see the colour in your cheeks again."

Clare said, "Ah . . . That must be the postman."

Daniel leaped to his feet, scrambled upstairs to the hall. A small white envelope with his name on it lay on the mat. He ripped it open. The glue was still damp.

Daniel, where have you been? I've missed you. Can we talk?
Jade

He flew over the road on wings.

Jesus, it was difficult.

Mum and I were giving Finn his tea in the kitchen, and Finn said, "Where's Dan?" for the umpteenth time.

Mum looked at me and said, "You'll have to tell Daniel, Jay. If you don't, it'll be all over between you. Is that what you want?"

I didn't say anything.

I picked Finn up, and we did a little dance together up the stairs, like we always do when it's bath time. The bath oil smelled of cut grass. I got in the bath with Finn and we made a huge, watery mess. Then I put him to bed, tucked him in snug and tight, and sang him a lullaby.

It always does the trick.

And all the time I was thinking about Daniel. His green eyes and all that wonderful inky-black hair. His skin beneath my hands in the garden.

I do like him. Well, actually, it's more than just like. I've been imagining us together, really together . . .

Of course, every time it happens, that feeling, I squash it down, look the other way, try to think about something else.

But it's there. I can't go on denying it.

So when Mum said, "Clare and Martin's car is back in their drive," my heart went *wham!* against my ribs.

I said, "Oh, is it?" like I couldn't care less, but then I roared up to my room and stared out, trying to get a glimpse of Daniel.

Mum put her head round the door.

"I've only got three words to say to you," she said.

"Oh, yeah?" I said, pretending to read a book.

"Go for it."

So I did.

Jade opened the door before he had time to ring the bell.

"Daniel." Her face was pale, but her eyes shone with relief.

"Hi." He wanted to take her in his arms, tell her how much he'd missed her.

"You got my note?"

"Yes. We've been walking in the Lakes . . . Martin needed a holiday. There didn't seem much point in my hanging around here—"

She cut rapidly in, "Look, I'm sorry. You took me by surprise. I'd no idea—"

"It's OK. I understand. I've been kicking myself. I should never have—"

"The thing is, you were right. *Laura* was right."

He felt frosty with shock. "You mean—"

"I *am* Finn's mum." Her voice was only for his ears. "It's just that we'd planned I'd never tell anyone, not until Finn was old enough to understand."

He flailed, tried to let her off the hook. "It's none of my business. You had every right to be angry."

Jade looked him in the eyes. She said, "But I *want* you to know."

He swallowed, overwhelmed by the compliment. "Are you sure?"

"Positive . . . I've thought of nothing else since you . . ."

He touched her cheek, she bent her head into his hand.

"Tonight," he murmured. "Let's go for a walk after tea."

"Right. Pick me up at seven."

Finn came racing through the hall. "'Lo, Dan!" he shouted. "You're back!"

"Hi, Finn!"

Daniel caught the child in his arms.

"Of course I'm back," he said.

He read bits of a science-fiction novel, played a computer game, ate, paced around his room, pulled up some garden lettuces for Clare, made treacle toffee which refused to set, drifted into sleep, woke with a start.

He counted the hours, willing the hands of his watch to move.

Then, finally, it was time and he dashed over the road.

Jade was waiting for him by the gate. Silently, he took her hand, saw her smile, bite her lip, felt her draw him closer.

They crossed Chalfont Road, turned left towards the

bridge and ran down to the narrow towpath. The canal lay still and quiet in the early evening light. Fishermen, trance-like, hunched over their rods, waiting for that flick of water, the curious, greedy mouth.

Jade asked, "When did Laura guess?"

"Remember in Blenheim, when Finn fell over?"

"Ah, yes." She pulled a leaf from the hedgerow, held it to her nose. "Those moments you can't plan for, you can't possibly arrange. They take you unawares." She smiled at Daniel, blushing at the look of love in his eyes. "And the truth slips out."

"Tell me all about it," he said.

So they walked down the towpath to Wolvercote and on to Port Meadow.

And she did.

Of course, I'd *rehearsed* the story so many times, but this was the first time I'd ever told anyone, apart from Mum and Dad.

Suddenly I was shaking with nerves. My hands were all clammy and I could feel cold sweat running down my back. I *so* wanted Daniel to go on liking me – and I didn't know whether he would when he heard what I'd done.

But I took a deep breath. I held on to Daniel's hand, although I couldn't look at him. I just wanted to say the words and keep on going until he knew everything.

Well, *almost* everything.

"Four years ago I fell in love."

My voice came out all thin and wobbly, but I didn't care.

"I was only thirteen. He was a lot older than me. He knew I had a crush on him. For a long time he tried not to notice me, brushed me aside whenever we met. But I couldn't get him out of my head. He became an obsession."

I felt Daniel's hand tighten round mine and our shoulders brushed and bumped as we walked.

"I've never told anybody who is he, not even Mum and Dad. If it had ever come out, his life would have been ruined.

We only had sex once and I never saw him again. He disappeared. He's got no idea he has a child – and I've no intention of telling him."

Daniel said quickly, "Don't you think the father has the right to know?"

"He's got no rights of any kind." I could feel the anger in me beginning to bubble up like it was coming from a well deep inside me that I'd put the lid on before Finn was born. "If he'd loved me, cared for me in any way, he'd never have disappeared like he did, without a word."

Daniel was silent, so I pushed on.

"At first, as the days went by and he never got in touch, I cried myself to sleep every night. Then I realised I might be pregnant. I went out and bought one of those pregnancy-testing kits . . . You should have seen the way the woman at the counter looked at me." She paused. "The test was positive, of course. Part of me couldn't believe it. I felt shocked, numb, glad, amazed, terrified – you name it. I felt everything all at the same time. My world changed overnight."

"You never thought of—"

"Having an abortion?"

The word hung in the air between us, dark and terrible.

"Sure, I *thought* about it. Before I told Mum and Dad, there were days when I was full of panic and fright, when I couldn't

see any other way out of the mess I'd got myself into." I
wanted to cry, remembering. "But I couldn't do it . . . not to
my own flesh and blood."

Daniel said quietly, "I'm glad."

I loved him so much for saying that. But I didn't give
anything away. I just went on walking and holding on to him.

"I decided I had to tell Mum and Dad. It was a Sunday in
January, early in the New Year. Dad was going back to
Brussels the next day, so I had a kind of deadline. We'd gone
for a walk after lunch in the snow on Primrose Hill. Kids
were whizzing around on their sledges, shouting for joy.
There was one little boy with bright red hair, sitting all
bunched up on an old tin tray, pushing his way down the hill.
I remember thinking, *In a few years' time, I'll be looking after a
child like that!* I suddenly felt so old! Full of new feelings of
responsibility . . . As if suddenly I'd lost my own childhood,
had it swallowed up in one huge gulp . . .

"Mum and Dad were fantastic. We sat on a bench at the
top of the hill and talked and talked. Then we found a café
and had pots of tea and soft buns with lemon icing. Funny the
details you remember."

I looked up at Daniel. He just said, "Go on," and swung his
arm around my shoulders.

"Dad wanted to know who the father was, but Mum told

him to stop pestering me. She gave me total support, right from the word go. She and Dad got married when she was only nineteen. She'd always wanted a huge family of her own. They'd hoped for more children, after me, but it didn't happen.

"So having Finn now, in a weird kind of way, is what they'd always wanted – even if he is mine!

"I said I couldn't go back to school. I couldn't face the questions and the gossip. I wanted to make a clean break. Mum said immediately we could go to France. We'd stayed once before in a holiday cottage in Brittany. I said, let's go back there. Nobody knew us, and until Finn was born we kept ourselves to ourselves. I did lots of school work at home with Mum.

"Finn was born in September. I stayed at home with him for the first four months and then in January I started at the local *lycée*. By that time me and Mum had settled Finn into a routine and we shared looking after him."

We walked across Port Meadow, to the river.

We watched a crew practising in a long-rowing boat, the hypnotic swing of their oars dipping in and out of the water; a golden retriever, sniffing and pattering about on the sand; geese strutting and preening in their feathery gangs.

He said, "I'm so glad you've told me."

"Do you feel differently about me?" I asked. "Now you know I'm a mum?"

I had to ask him. I had to know whether I'd ruined everything between us.

He hugged me. I could see tears in his eyes.

He said, "There are still a thousand questions I want to ask you. But there'll be plenty of time for them."

"Yes," I said.

I watched him looking out over the river.

I thought, *But you haven't answered* my *question.*

Do you still want me now you know what I've done?

Sweet of the boy to buy me yellow roses.

He came for lunch the Saturday after he got back from Windermere.

When he'd gone, I put one of the roses in my copy of the first book Daddy ever wrote, crushed it flat and beautiful, to remember.

Said he was sorry!

"Nothing to be sorry for," I said, but he brushed that aside. Said I'd taken the wind out of his sails, he'd never thought of Jade like that, wondered how he could have been so blind.

Then he said, "You were right. I plucked up the courage to ask Jade, like you told me to. She went ballistic, shrieked at me like there was no tomorrow. She threw me out of the garden, hysterical. When I looked back at her, she was sobbing, and Finn ran up to her and started to cry too. I couldn't get the sight of both of them, like that, and all because of me, out of my head."

When he'd got back from the Lakes, Jade had thought better of the pretence. Decided to spill the beans, told Daniel about what had happened.

But she's keeping the father a secret . . .

I'm glad I know.

I'm glad I was right.

But I'm getting very worried about the boy.

Has he *any* idea what he's letting himself in for?

Can Jade be trusted? Is she just using him because he's such a sweetie? Will she ditch him when she's had enough or found someone else?

You can tell me I'm seeing the black side if you like.

The black swans.

Maybe I am.

But it doesn't stop me worrying like hell.

And I wish I'd been wrong . . .

Daniel

The rain pounded on to grey pavements and sodden gardens.

For two days, sulky skies loured over Oxford. Clare grumbled about another wet August, wondered where summer had vanished. Leaves on the heavy trees in Chalfont Road sighed and dripped. Some began to fall.

Reluctantly, the rain swallowed and stopped. Tuesday dawned fresh and clear, without apology. People splashed their way to work.

Jade said, "The garden's still much too wet to play in. Let's go into Oxford this afternoon. Mum's given me a list of things to buy. We can wheel Finn in his pushchair. I'll bring him to yours after nursery. He needs new shoes — and so do I!"

Daniel stared down at his old trainers. "Suppose I do too. These got soaked yesterday. There are shoe shops on every corner in Oxford. We'll be spoiled for choice . . . And there's a great group of buskers we could listen to. They come every summer. I spotted them again last week."

The city heaved with shoppers, grateful for the hint of sunshine and clear skies. Droves of tourists obediently listened in a droopy fashion to their guides, blocking the paths. Daniel took Jade's arm. He steered her and Finn through the clusters of bodies onto Cornmarket, noticing how Finn's olive skin and dark curls attracted admiring glances.

In a way still strange to him, he felt proud to be with them, protective of their safety – and now a guardian of their secret.

The musicians were busking on a corner near the Covered Market, as usual. They were well rehearsed, played with vigour and confidence: something classical that Daniel vaguely recognised but could not name. The music cut sharply through the bustling hum, adding to the trudge of footsteps the sound of elegance and style.

Finn waved a fist in their direction, pointing, demanding to be let out of his chair so he could see.

Jade bent to deal with the harness. She lifted Finn into her arms. They stood as a group in the middle of the gathering crowd, listening and looking. People threw coins into a damp, upturned beret. The coins chinked to the music. Fascinated, Finn stared, crowing with delight, drumming his fist to the beat.

Daniel watched the musicians: two girls, two men, slim, young, dressed casually in jeans. Identical bright red scarves twined around their necks. Three of them held delicate violins. They smiled to each other as they played, their heads bobbing, their fingers dancing.

One of the musicians played a flute. He had olive skin and dark hair pulled into a smooth ponytail. Intent on the tune, his body swayed to the rhythm, his feet tapped. His eyes, a startling pale blue, gazed into the sea of faces, then upwards to the sky. And then across to Daniel – and down to Jade and the bundle in her arms.

The flautist's eyes burned with astonishment. His mouth faltered, slackened, gaped. The pure notes of the flute died in midstream as his arms fell to his sides. The violinists glanced at him questioningly, but their beat never wavered and they soldiered on.

In an instant Jade had turned to face Daniel. One hand clutched him fiercely, the nails bit. He winced with pain. She pushed Finn into his arms.

She whispered, "Quick! We must get away from here. Don't ask me why . . . Just move!"

She shoved her way through the crowd, reached a gap, raced away from him up the narrow side street, wildly trundling the pushchair ahead of her. Daniel followed, Finn heavy in his arms. The child thought this was a marvellous new game and squealed with laughter.

Jade had vanished. She'd turned the corner into the Covered Market and stood with her back against the wall.

Daniel caught her up. "Are you OK?"

She was pale, shaking with shock. "Of course not."

"What's the matter?" Daniel stared at her anxiously. She looked as if she were about to faint. "Tell me, quickly."

"I never thought I'd see him again."

"Who?" Daniel propped Finn into his pushchair and strapped him in, cursing his fumbling fingers. He lowered his voice. "*Who* have you seen?"

"Who d'you think?" Jade ran a hand through her hair. Her lips scarcely moved.

"The buskers?"

Jade nodded. "The guy playing the flute."

"You know him?"

"It's Kieran. Kieran McVeigh." Her voice was a mere breath of air. "Here, in Oxford. I can't believe it. It was like seeing a ghost."

Her hands flew to her face, covered her eyes. The words fluttered into the murky shadows of the passageway, hung there like watchful bats.

"Who *is* he?"

The question seemed to echo around the market. But even as he asked it, his mouth filling with the bitter taste of jealousy and dread, he knew the answer.

"He's Finn's dad."

Daniel took Jade's icy hands in his. "Did he see you?"

Jade nodded, her body trembling. "I know he did . . . I'm sure of it . . . It's why he stopped playing."

"D'you think he saw Finn?"

"He *must* have done. I was holding Finn in my arms, pointing the musicians out to him."

Daniel said wildly, "Loads of other people were milling about—"

Jade shook her head. "It's like I was *showing* him his own child! Holding him up to be admired . . . I couldn't have made it any clearer if I'd tried."

"Then you think Kieran might have realised Finn's his son?"

Jade stared at Daniel. "They're the spitting image of each other – their hair, their eyes . . . God, Daniel. What am I going to do?"

Daniel took control.

He smoothed Jade's hair, stroked her shoulder. He pulled the handle of the pushchair towards him and locked her fingers over it.

"Go and sit in there," he nodded towards the corner café. "Buy yourself a strong cup of tea. Get one for me. Put lots of sugar in it. Give Finn a drink and a biscuit. I'll go back and see if Kieran and the group are still playing."

"What if they are?"

"Then at least we'll know where he is."

Slowly, as if she hardly knew what she was doing, walking as if with wooden limbs, Jade wheeled Finn into the café. Daniel made sure they were safely inside and waved to her through the window. Then, rapidly, he threaded his way back towards Cornmarket.

He could hear the clatter of bicycles, a delivery van parking outside the market, men shouting instructions, the squeal of mobile phones, the babble of traffic and voices: but now it was as if they came from a distant planet, as if the world had changed and darkened, as if the sounds were dampened by the wild thumping of his heart.

The crowd on the corner of the street were listening and looking in a different way too. He could see their faces. They were nudging each other, laughing at an act. The piping notes of the music had been drowned out. Before he even reached the corner, Daniel knew the musicians had gone.

In their place wobbled a man on a pair of stilts. He was disguised as a ghost: sheets flapped clumsily around his body. A skull-mask covered his face. Through it his eyes shone with lunatic glee. He was juggling with oranges, scattering the bright fruit high into the air, catching each one in his whitened hands, shooting them up again.

Daniel shivered. A wave of premonition flooded through him. There was something revolting about this apparition, as grotesque and absurd as the musicians had been vivid and beautiful. Yet if he and Jade had arrived ten minutes later, maybe this strange creature's crowd-pulling bravado is all they would have seen.

And Kieran would still be a ghost from Jade's past.

Daniel walked slowly back to the café.

He realised with a shock how much he wanted Kieran to disappear again, to stay out of their lives. He must be thirty years old – maybe older.

Jade had been *thirteen*.

The word *paedophile* lurched across Daniel's mind. A wave of nausea gripped his stomach, making him feel dizzy. Had Jade really wanted Kieran that much? Or had she been seduced? Had he forced her, or tricked her . . . Did he make a habit of seducing little girls?

What if Jade had been just one in a long line of virgin conquests?

Was that why he'd vanished so abruptly?

To move on to the next?

I sat down in the café, shaking.

The cups rattled on the saucers, the tea slopped every-where. I couldn't control my hands.

I gave Finn a chocolate biscuit, kept half an eye on him as the memories came pouring back.

Kieran.

He looked a lot older and thinner. His eyes seemed to have lost some of their sparkle. I felt like screaming at him, *Where have you been? Why did you disappear? Have you thought about me for a single moment since that night?*

The man who turned into a reptile, sliding away to vanish for ever in burning grains of sand.

He'd shone with delight at our perfomance.

How we'd rehearsed that concert, right from the very first week of term, from his arrival as our new music teacher. Every note, every phrase, every song, every chorus. Over and over, until we'd got as close to perfection as we ever would.

But that night, we surpassed ourselves. Pulled out all the stops.

Didn't he just know how to get the best from us!

Stand properly . . . Stand tall . . . Relax . . . Breathe . . . Fill those lungs . . . Use every ounce of your bodies . . . Right . . . Excellent . . . Now sing for me as if you were larks flying through the blue sky into heaven.

And we did. I sang a solo for him, a song he'd written specially for the concert. He called it "Nightingale".

God, it was so good.

Mum and Dad had to be in Brussels. They couldn't be there to hear me. They never knew what they'd missed. I told them I'd be staying the weekend with my best friend.

Maybe if they *had* been there, Kieran and I, we'd never have . . .

After the concert, we were all standing in a group.

One by one, everybody else seemed to drift away. Until it was only Kieran and me.

He said, "Well, now, Jade . . . How are you getting home?"

"I'm not sure."

"Would you like a lift? I can't leave you to face the streets of Camden Town. Not on your own, not on a Saturday night."

I said yes.

But I thought, *Yes, please, before I die of wanting you.*

I knew the house would be empty, that I would ask him in.

99

Apart from me giving him directions to where I lived, we said nothing to each other in the car, not a single word. He parked a few houses down from mine.

Then he said, "Well, Jade. I'll have to be the gentleman and see you to the door."

We stood on the step and looked at each other.

He said, "Goodnight is it, then, my nightingale?"

That beautiful Irish voice entirely melted my heart.

"No," I said. "Not yet."

And I reached up and kissed him on the mouth.

After that, I hardly remember . . .

"What d'you mean, none of them are there?" Jade's hand shook, her tea slopped into the saucer. "They can't have disappeared into thin air."

He slid into the seat opposite. "There's no sign of them."

"But that's impossible. We only left them five minutes ago."

"They must've decided to go home."

"Because of me?"

"He certainly stopped playing when he saw you." He shrugged. "I don't know, Jade. Maybe they'd been busking for hours and they'd had enough." He didn't want to tell her about the juggler-ghost – or how the word *paedophile* seemed to be sucking at his thoughts like a leech. "Maybe it was time for another act to take over."

"You don't think . . ."

"What?"

"That Kieran *followed* us?"

Daniel glanced around the café. Two elderly ladies gossiped in a corner, putting the world to rights. One of them started smiling at Finn and playing peek-a-boo. A student sat scribbling over a tattered set of notes. A young family ate their way through a pile of toasted teacakes.

"Well, he's not in here." He tried to make her lighten up. "And I haven't spotted him peering at us through that window with a magnifying glass."

Jade shook her head. "This isn't funny, Daniel."

His tea tasted of black treacle. He swilled it down. "There's no need to snap my head off."

"I didn't mean—"

"How do you think *I* feel?" Self-pity stabbed a fist into his stomach. "I don't want to see Kieran —" the name stuck in his throat — "any more than you do. What do you think it's like for me, imagining you with him?" He wanted to say, *And spoiling everything between us*, but he bit back the words.

"I'm *sorry*." Her face was red and puffy.

"Look." He forced himself to be calm. "I think we should pretend that nothing's happened. Let's do the shopping, get it over as fast as possible."

"Can't we just go home?"

"Your mum will wonder why we're empty-handed. Do you want to tell her about Kieran?"

Jade bit her lip. "After all these years of keeping his identity a secret?"

"So if you don't want her to know, we'll have to pretend

this is an ordinary afternoon." He reached across the table, warmed her hands in his. "Let's think this out, Jade. What's the worst that could happen?"

Her eyes flickered at him. "I don't want to see Kieran again. Not ever. He dumped me as if I'd done something terrible, not loved him, given myself to him in a way I never had before . . . And never have since."

His heart thumped with jealousy – and a swirl of crazy relief.

"Look, if Kieran's living in Oxford, if he's seen you, recognised you – and realised that Finn could be his child – you may *have* to face him again."

Tears filled her eyes. "I know."

"But I'll be there for you." He took a deep breath. "I'm not chickening out of our relationship because that creep has returned to haunt you."

"You won't? You promise?"

He kissed her fingertips. "I promise."

Finn laughed up at them from his pushchair. He started to sing "Baa, baa, black sheep" at the top of his voice. He'd smeared his face with chocolate.

"Oh, Finn, what a mess you're in," Jade said. She glanced at Daniel. The corners of her mouth dipped. "Just like your mum."

*

At her garden gate, Jade said, "Can I ask you a big favour?"

"Name it."

"Would you go back there tonight? To Cornmarket? See if the group are playing?"

"And then what?"

"Wait until they've finished for the evening and follow Kieran home? . . . I'd feel safer if I knew where he lives."

"What good's *that* going to do?"

"I don't know . . . He might just be visiting friends, or he might be around for good. I need to find out – without him seeing me."

He said reluctantly, "If you insist. I'll ask Clare for an early tea, in case it takes me all evening."

"And if you don't see him tonight?"

"Give me a chance . . . One step at a time."

Jade hugged him fiercely. "Kiss me."

She reached up to him. He closed his eyes.

He trudged into Oxford. The rain, back with a vengeance, flounced spitefully into his face; his new trainers scraped against his heels.

I just hope Kieran's on the corner . . . If he is, I wonder how long I'll have to stand in the rain . . . I might have to jump on a bus to follow him . . . What if he has a car? . . . I haven't thought any of this through.

But the weather had frightened most people away. Cornmarket gaped emptily back at him. Neither juggling stilted ghosts nor musicians played on the corner of the street.

Back at Clare and Martin's, he stripped off his wet clothes and dried his hair. He rang Jade, told her he'd drawn a blank. He said it would be pretty pointless going back the following afternoon. But Jade put up so many reasons, practically begging him, that he finally agreed.

This time he was lucky – if you could call it that.

He heard the musicians from the corner of Broad Street. He followed their trail of notes by slipping along Cornmarket, close to the shops on the left-hand side, so Kieran couldn't possibly spot him. Then, swiftly, he doubled back into a side street and emerged behind the group.

On the dot of six o'clock the music stopped.

Daniel wrenched himself out of a reverie, stared at the group with his back against the wall. One of the violinists picked up the beret; money clinked. Kieran slipped his flute into a slim felt bag. The others packed away their instruments, stood talking in low voices. They shook hands, hugged each other. One of the girls wound a long green scarf around her neck.

They left in different directions.

Kieran stood for a moment on his own. He pulled a scarlet sweater over his head, lit a cigarette, dragged at it, smoothed a hand over his ponytail. Holding the flute, he bobbed quickly across Cornmarket, turned left into George Street, ducked into a newsagent's and emerged carrying a newspaper.

Daniel followed, keeping his distance.

Kieran crossed the street. He hesitated outside the cinema, checking the posters, then his watch. He moved rapidly on.

Daniel breathed a sigh of relief.

He's walking towards the station. If he buys a ticket, how will I know where he's going? How do private investigators do it?

Kieran reached the crossroads. The traffic stopped him in his tracks; the lights changed from red to green. He crossed the road at the bottom of Hythe Bridge Street, battling against a tide of commuters who had flooded off the latest train.

A hand grasped Daniel's arm. He jumped.

Laura said, "Daniel! Fancy bumping into you!"

"Hi, Laura."

Shit! Talk about bad timing . . .

He wrenched his gaze away from Keiran's disappearing back. Laura looked amazingly smart. She wore a pale summer trouser-suit with a white shirt, and carried a battered briefcase.

"I've just been to London, to see Humphrey. I've got a contract to celebrate."

"Congratulations."

He craned his neck to see over her shoulder. The scarlet sweater had been gobbled up in the throng.

He must be behind that stream of people, over there, crossing the bridge . . . I could've got really close to him if it hadn't been for Laura . . .

"What's the matter? Who are you looking for?"

Daniel muttered sullenly, "I was meant to be meeting someone . . ."

"And they haven't turned up?"

He thrust his hands into his pockets. The crowd on the bridge had thinned.

Like a burst bubble, Kieran had vanished into the air.

"No. Don't suppose there's much point now in my hanging around."

"Right, then," Laura said firmly. "Come and have supper."

"In Woodstock?" He bit back his irritation. "I'm not sure, Laura—"

"No, let's find somewhere nice in Oxford. I'm going to push the boat out. To celebrate." She took his arm. "You look half starved. Come on, you can eat your way through the menu. We'll ring Clare from the restaurant, tell her where you are."

Daniel called round at nine o'clock, much later than I'd hoped.

All evening I'd been thinking, *He's late, he must have found Kieran, followed him. He must know a lot by now. I can't wait to see him. Why doesn't he ring?*

But he'd nothing interesting to report. He was late because he'd bumped into Laura, had to have supper with her. He'd lost Kieran in the crowd.

"I'm so sorry," he said. "I feel like a prat. I hope you don't feel I've let you down."

"Of course not . . . Thanks for trying . . . But there's no point in trying again . . . I'm sure you've better things to do with your time."

I tried not to show how fed up I felt. Angry and frightened at the same time.

Poor Daniel. He walked back across the road looking so miserable. It's not *his* fault I'm in such a mess. I shouldn't take it out on him. I'm going to make a big effort to be nice to him, not to talk about Kieran, to pretend that nothing's happened.

But inside me, I'm dead scared. I know Kieran's seen us — Finn and me — and I've got a nasty feeling things aren't going to end here.

In fact, they might be just beginning.

I'll have to watch Finn like a hawk. Not that I don't anyway, but you know, keep a really close eye on him. Just in case.

Mum spotted something was wrong. At first, after Daniel left, I said, "It's nothing, honest. I'm just a bit tired."

But then I thought, *This is crazy. What if Kieran finds out where I live, comes to the door, tries to see me? Asks about Finn?*

Mum has a right to know.

So that evening I sat down with her and told her about Kieran. Well, not everything, but I told her his name, who he was, how we'd met, what he looked like. How Daniel and I had seen him busking in Cornmarket, that maybe he'd moved to Oxford and was living here permanently.

Ironic, isn't it? Mum and I went to live in France not only to be nearer to Dad but mostly to escape Kieran. Him and my school and all the wretched gossip. Now we haven't been back in England for more than five minutes and — what do you know? — Kieran's staring me in the face.

Mum was great. I mean, at first she was so furious that it had been my music teacher, I thought she was going to explode all over the kitchen floor. "If parents can't trust *teachers*," she said, "who *can* we trust? Men like that should be put behind bars for life."

But I told her the truth.

"I wanted it to happen," I said. "It was the night of the concert. You thought I was staying the weekend with Alison. I wasn't. I didn't. I was home alone and I wanted Kieran to be with me."

After a bit she calmed down. She said she was really glad I'd told her – that I wasn't to worry about anything. She'd have to tell Dad, but they were both right behind me. And I was to let her know if I saw Kieran again, keep her in touch with what was going on.

Made me promise I wouldn't tackle this alone.

I could tell she was worried.

She wasn't letting on, but I could tell.

Daniel

He became aware that he was beginning to worry about Jade.

All the time. Not just when he saw her, when they were together, when they had Finn under their nose. Then he could make her laugh – it was an effort, but he tried – make sure she knew he was on her side, watching out for her.

It was worse when they were apart. Then his imagination took over. His fears stopped him sleeping. When he did drift off, they haunted his dreams.

What if Kieran comes back into Jade's life full-time? Maybe she'll decide to go off with him and take Finn with her. What if I never see her again?

But Jade remained adamant: she didn't want to see Kieran again. For several days she even refused to talk about him. She tried to pretend the Cornmarket episode had never happened, brushed it aside, changed the subject when Daniel mentioned it.

But one evening he and Jade were alone in the house, baby-sitting Finn while Eve was out. Jade knelt on her hands and knees, clearing Finn's toys from the living-room floor.

Daniel said, "Tell me about Kieran."

"Why?"

"Because I need to know."

"I just want to forget all about it. It's over and done with."

"It can't ever be that, can it? I mean, I had a girlfriend last year. Polly and I went out for a couple of months. But we never got really close." Daniel blushed. "We never even had sex, and we just sort of ground to a halt. Polly and I are over and done with. I might never see her again – and even if I do, we'll only be distant friends. But Kieran will always be a part of your life because of Finn."

Jade sat back on her heels. "I suppose you're right. So . . . what do you want to know?"

"Tell me about him from the beginning . . . How did you meet?"

Her eyes flickered in the evening light. "He was my school's new music teacher."

Daniel gasped. "But you were thirteen!"

"Why do you think I tried so hard to protect his identity? I knew if the school ever found out about us, he'd be sacked on the spot."

"Serve him right!" The words burst out of Daniel as if he were spitting fire.

Grimly, Jade nodded. "The police would've been on to

him, the press would've got hold of the story. They'd have made the connection with me, even if I had tried to keep out of it – and they'd never have given him a second chance. His whole life would've been ruined."

Daniel clenched his fists, wanting to punch Kieran's face. "It *should* have been!" He took a deep breath to steady his voice. "So what happened?"

"Kieran arrived the first day of the autumn term. The head introduced him at assembly. We had to sing a hymn – and usually we sounded like rubbish. Kieran told us how to stand, how to breathe. Then he began to conduct. It was magic, like he'd shot a bolt of electricity through the hall and we'd been fired up with it."

She bit her lip, remembering.

"We sang like angels. I'd never have believed it. Guys in my class who'd never bothered to open their mouths, sounding like angels."

"Had *you* sung before Kieran arrived?" He wanted to see her as she had been, at thirteen, in her school uniform, her hair down to her shoulders, sounding like an angel.

"I'd always adored singing. I had one of the best voices in my class, couldn't wait for singing lessons. The minute Kieran arrived, they became the highlight of my week."

He asked sharply, "Did he know you had a crush on him?"

"Maybe not at first." Jade blushed. "I fought against it. I kept telling myself he probably had a girlfriend, that I was being an idiot. But I was well and truly hooked."

"So how did you get to know him? It couldn't have been easy!"

"He asked me to sing a solo at the Christmas concert, on the Saturday before term ended. He wrote a song for it. He played the flute accompaniment."

"Was he making a pass at you when he asked?"

"I honestly don't think he was. Lots of us auditioned. I was desperate to be chosen — and beside myself with joy when I was."

"And you brought the house down, right?"

Jade laughed. "We'd rehearsed until we were note perfect." Her eyes grew misty with memories. "I used to watch his face as he played the flute for me . . ."

Daniel swallowed back a surge of jealousy. "He must have known how you felt."

"I didn't spell it out, but it was probably written all over me . . . That night, after the concert, he drove me home. I knew the house would be empty. That's when . . ."

Daniel shifted in his chair, trying unsuccessfully to stop imagining Jade in Kieran's arms; Kieran in Jade's childish bedroom, pressing her down against her single bed . . .

"What happened afterwards?"

"Kieran drove back to his flat at three in the morning. I spent Sunday in a daze. Mum was in Brussels with Dad for an important dinner. She thought I was staying with a friend."

"So later that Sunday . . . did Kieran ring you?"

Jade lifted her pale face to look at him. "I never spoke to him again."

Daniel frowned. "Didn't you have school on the Monday?"

"We had four more days to the end of term. Kieran never turned up. At first I thought he'd had an accident driving back to his flat. Then the head told us there was something wrong with one of his family, an emergency, he'd been called home. And he wouldn't be coming back."

"And you thought it must have been because of you?"

"Of course. If he'd had to leave unexpectedly, he could have sent me *some* kind of message: a letter, a phone call. Anything. The silence was terrible."

"Did you try to find him?"

"On the last day of term, I went to his flat in West Hampstead. I got his address from the school secretary. I'd bought him a Christmas card and got everyone in the class to sign it. I said I'd send it – but I knew I was going to deliver it myself. I put a scrap of paper inside, with my phone number and three words: *Please ring me* . . . He never did."

"And he wasn't at the flat?"

"No. I rang the bell, but nobody answered. I hung about in the freezing cold. Some newspapers sat on the porch with two bottles of milk. I waited and waited. I knew it was hopeless, but I didn't want to leave."

She gave a short laugh.

"Then one of his neighbours started peering up at me from the basement. I didn't want her coming out, asking who I was. So I shoved the card through the door, threw the papers into a dustbin, picked up one of the bottles to throw that away too. It was half frozen to the ground and it smashed. Milk slopped all over my feet. I stared down at it and thought, *That's just what I'm doing . . . Crying over spilt milk.*" She looked up at him, her face flushed, her eyes full of tears. "The end of the big affair."

"Not just an end." Daniel reached for her. "A beginning."

"Yes."

For a moment, she clung to him. Then she stood up. From his room, Finn had started to wail for attention. "Out of bad always comes good. Isn't that what they say?"

Sometimes I have a weird feeling when I wake up.

About the kind of day I'm going to have: good or bad, easy or difficult, ordinary or peculiar. The morning after Daddy had died in the night, I knew at once, the minute I opened my eyes, that something terrible had happened. There was a kind of ghastly silence in the cottage, palpable, you could touch it, feel it, like it was dripping off the walls. I felt so cold I could hardly move my arms and legs.

But this morning I woke up feeling on top of the world. Rushed blithely around, feeding the animals, planning the food I was going to buy for the boy's lunch tomorrow. Clipped Barnaby's lead round his neck, with him raring to go.

That's exactly the word for it. Raring. Tugging like mad, off down Chaucer's Lane, like we always do. Then I pulled him left towards the shops, instead of right into Blenheim. Needed the butcher's first, then the supermarket.

Barnaby hates shops because I have to tie him up outside. Makes a huge fuss, as if I'm going to leave him there for months. Sits there looking as doleful as a wet sock, his head slumped on his paws. Everyone who passes says, "Ah, poor doggie," which only makes him feel more sorry for himself than ever.

So we were standing there, him heaving to go to Blenheim, me pulling towards the shops, when *whack!* the lead snapped.

I knew it was rotten, I'd been meaning to replace it for weeks. But that stupid blithering pooch thinks I'm letting him off the hook, he can't believe his luck. He went roaring off into the road.

The van couldn't possibly have stopped in time.

Screech of brakes, a single frightful howl from my darling Barnaby.

Silence.

I uncovered my eyes, threw myself across the road. He was half under one of the wheels. I screamed, "Get off him, get the hell off him," but even when the driver did, I knew it was no good. I looked into Barnaby's eyes and all he said was, "Help, I think I'm done for."

I picked him up and staggered down to the bottom of Chaucer's Lane, round the corner to the place where I park my car. I was shaking and sobbing. Several people called, "Are you OK?" Someone else shouted my name from across the street, but I didn't stop.

I managed to get the car door open. I put him on the back

seat, sat in the front and tried to stop shaking like a leaf. Barnaby was whimpering like a child. It was the saddest sound I've ever heard.

I drove as fast as I could to the vet. Mr Frindlesham has a practice in Yarnton. Known him for years, sweet man, handles any animal you care to name. They can be wild as tigers, Frinny calms them down just by being near them.

He said, "You'll have to leave Barnaby with us, Laura . . . It's bad, but I'll try to patch him up."

"And if you can't?"

He said, "I'll do my best, Laura . . . Give me a couple of hours. I'll ring you. Go home and have a cup of tea. Clean yourself up."

I looked down at my cotton frock.

It was covered in blood.

Daniel

He knew at once something was wrong.

Laura's front door gaped half open. He pushed at it, calling her name. He stepped into the hall and shut the door. Muffin curled around his legs, her tail high, mewing.

The cottage was strangely quiet. Then he realised: there'd been no welcoming bark from Barnaby.

He called for Laura more loudly.

Her voice came flat and quiet. "I'm in here, in Daddy's room."

She still wore her pyjamas, slumped at the table, her hair wild and sticky. Her mouth seemed to be bruised and bitten. Dark shadows stained the skin beneath her eyes.

She looked at Daniel. "It was all my fault."

"What's wrong?"

"Barnaby's dead. It happened yesterday."

"*What?*"

"The vet tried to operate, but Barnaby died before he could finish. It was the van, see? The wheels of the van. Crushed Barnaby's insides."

Daniel knelt beside her. "I'm so sorry, Laura."

"I know you are. That leather lead. Rotten. Should have replaced it. Snapped. Blithering pooch —" she'd started to cry again — "dashed into the road. Driver. Couldn't stop. Wasn't his fault. All mine."

"Oh, Laura. Don't blame yourself."

She wiped her face with a sodden handkerchief. "But I do. Look at me. Useless. Not dressed. Supposed to give you lunch. No food in the house. Not done any shopping."

"We'll go out instead." He gave her a brief hug. "Go and have a bath, get dressed."

"Could you feed Muffin for me? She can't understand why her number one enemy isn't here to fight."

"Of course."

He watched as Laura stumbled up the stairs.

In the kitchen, dirty plates and cups littered the draining-board. He filled Muffin's bowl with her favourite dry biscuits, stroked her as she crouched over the food, her head on one side, crunching.

Then he washed Barnaby's dish, dried it and stacked it away, out of sight, in a corner cupboard.

Poor old, dear old Barnaby.

I'll miss him.

Everything feels like it's going horribly wrong . . .

*

On Monday morning he cycled into Oxford, padlocked his bike in St Giles. He crossed Broad Street and turned right, up the Turl.

If the musicians were playing, he wanted to avoid them. He had other things on his mind.

He turned right again and ducked into the Covered Market, quiet and empty at the start of another week. The pet-food shop was at the top of a passageway. He pushed at the door. The pungent smell of animal feed filled the air.

"What can I get you?" An assistant with frizzy ginger hair and pea-green overalls smiled across at him.

"I haven't come to buy anything." He moved towards her. "Sorry. I just wanted some advice."

"Go ahead, sonny. Ask away."

"A friend of mine, her basset hound was run over last week. I was thinking about buying a replacement. Where's the best place to go?"

The woman paused from measuring birdseed into a paper bag. "If you want a pedigree, it'll cost you a small fortune."

"What about something a bit more ordinary?"

"There's the Blue Cross near Burford. They always have pets who need good homes. You'll have to pay them something, of course, prove you can be a good owner. But that's where I'd go if I were you."

"Right. Thank you."

A man with dark hair had flashed past the window. Behind Daniel's back, the door opened and closed. But when he turned to leave, the shop was empty.

"Thank you very much," he said again, bleakly, to fill the gap.

He left the shop, checked carefully left and right. Every passageway stood deserted. He shivered. The hair on his neck crawled with sudden alarm.

I think I'm being watched.

He walked back towards St Giles, trying not to look over his shoulder. He kept on, at the same brisk pace, even when the footsteps behind him ran to catch him up.

A voice with a soft, seductive Irish lilt said, "Excuse me . . . Please, won't you wait a moment? . . . I need to talk to you."

Daniel stopped in his tracks and turned.

Kieran stood in front of him, tall, thin, almost stooped. His face was unnervingly like Finn's.

So this is him.

"I hope you won't mind." The blue eyes glittered at him fiercely.

Daniel said curtly, "What do you want?"

"I hope you won't think I'm being terribly rude, accosting you like this." The voice was faintly sarcastic. "I need to ask you something."

Pretend you've never seen him before. "Who *are* you?"

"Oh, come *on*, don't start playing games! You know who I am."

"I've never seen you before . . ."

Kieran grasped his arm. "You're lying. My name's McVeigh. Kieran McVeigh. I play the flute. I saw you last week. You were with Jade —" he said the name with a gentle lingering — "and that beautiful wee child."

Daniel wrenched free of Kieran's grip. "I've no idea what you're on about."

"Oh, I think you do. I've been following you, young man. I know where Jade lives. And you live opposite her house."

Daniel panicked. "So what if I do?"

"Ah." Kieran gave a deep sigh, his shoulders relaxed. He reached into his jeans for a packet of cigarettes. "Now we're getting somewhere . . . Will you have a smoke with me?"

"No. And if you don't mind, I've got things to do."

Kieran blocked his way. "I'm *sure* you have, young man." Again the sarcasm. "But you see, this is really important. I mean *really* . . . I have to see Jade, I have to talk to her . . .

I don't mean her any harm." He lit a cigarette and sucked into it, the fingers of his right hand stained brown-yellow with nicotine. His eyes scanned Daniel's face. "You do believe me, don't you?"

The hint of mockery in Kieran's question was like a flame to a puddle of petrol. Anger flooded through Daniel.

"You've had plenty of time to talk. Years of it. But you dumped her, didn't you? And now it's too late."

"I see you know quite a lot about me." Kieran blew a trail of smoke into Daniel's face.

He clenched his fists. *I'd like to thump him, smack between the eyes.* "Why don't you get the hell out of here and leave her alone?"

"I'm afraid that's out of the question. I must see her. And it's urgent."

"What's any of this got to do with me?"

"I want you to help me, man to man."

"And why should I do that?"

"You're her boyfriend, aren't you? I assume you *care* about her?"

"More than *you* ever will, that's for sure!"

"*There* . . . I knew you'd be a clever young man and agree."

"I haven't said yes to anything!"

"But you will, won't you?"

Daniel took a deep breath. He was beginning to feel sick.

"Look . . . Just what *do* you want?"

"It's so simple . . . Give Jade a message from me."

"Which is?"

"I have to see her. Tonight. I'll be waiting outside Blackwell's. The main bookshop, opposite the Radcliffe. I'll be there on the dot of six o'clock. Will you tell her that?"

The blue eyes had lost their glitter. Now they were begging for help.

"I can't promise anything."

Kieran dragged at the cigarette, filled his lungs with its fumes, flung it on the pavement, ground his heel into it. His eyes never left Daniel's face.

"Thank you, young man. I'm much obliged to you."

He turned away.

Daniel stood there, his legs shaking, his heart thumping with rage. He watched Kieran disappear down the Turl, the arrogant swagger of his hips, the impertinent swing of his ponytail. A dark patch of sweat on his T-shirt spread between his shoulder blades as if he'd been caught in the rain.

Bastard.

What the hell am I going to do?

I might have guessed that Kieran wouldn't simply go away.

Four years ago, I'd have given my right arm to hear from him, cried myself to sleep with the pain of his silence.

Now I just want him out of my life. But I know he isn't going to leave me alone.

After Daniel left last week, after I'd spent what felt like hours talking about Kieran — and it wasn't easy, putting all those memories into words — the phone rang.

When I answered it, the voice said, "Would that be Jade?"

I dropped the receiver as if it were on fire. *Slam!* Then I took it off the hook again, so he couldn't call me back, ran into the kitchen and shut the door to get as far away from the phone as possible.

After all those years of silence, that beautiful soft Irish voice ringing in my head. *"Would that be Jade?"*

Well, no, it wouldn't be.

Not the Jade he knew.

That silly little girl with only one thought in her head: to sing for him like an angel, prove how much she loved him, make him love her. Grew up overnight, she did, the moment she realised she was going to have his child.

The next day, Friday, he had the nerve to come to the door. Not that I answered it. I was taking Finn to nursery. Mum told me afterwards. She hadn't let on that she knew who he was. Just said she'd pass on the message. That a friend of Jade's was in Oxford and wanted to see her.

Kieran McVeigh.

Please leave me alone.

What'll I do if you don't?

Having the boy around most of the weekend helped a lot.

He's a diamond. He cleaned the place up a bit, took me out to eat. Fed Muffin. We walked in Blenheim, though it was very strange without Barnaby. I kept feeling there was something missing, something I should be doing. I wasn't being heaved around and I couldn't get used to it.

But of course he had to go back to Clare and Martin's, and I knew I had to pull myself together on my own. Had to face the week without him. Had to get on with Daddy's book.

On Monday I said to myself, right, go round the cottage and get rid of everything that reminds you of that stupid blithering pooch. Dog hair on the carpet? Hoover it up. Dog food in the cupboards? Chuck it in the bin. Chewed-up toys under the stairs? Pack them away. I did it all like a bloody robot. Never a tear fell from my eye.

Then that evening as I collapsed on to the sofa, something uncomfortable dug into my back. I rooted it out. There in my hand was an old bone Barnaby had buried for safe keeping.

That finished me off. I was in floods. Muffin gave me one

of her long hard stares. Then she crept on to my lap, bless her, to comfort me.

I kept on thinking, first I'd lost *her*, then Daddy, now my one and only Barnaby.

What if anything happens to the boy? What if he runs off with Jade, or gets hurt in an accident – or just decides he can't be bothered to see me again?

How will I cope?

Daniel

He pedalled like mad back to Clare and Martin's, arrived sweaty and puffing.

He crashed up to his room, stared at the pinboard and his precious photograph, bent double to calm the stitch in his side. But there was nothing he could do to calm the thoughts which flung themselves around his head like bats in a belfry.

If I don't pass on the message, and there are repercussions, Jade'll say it's all my bloody fault. I'll feel guilty: I kind of promised Kieran I would.

But if I do tell Jade and she still won't speak to him, I'll have to go back and tell him.

He'll probably kill me.

On the other hand, if she meets him again, she may decide she's still in love with the guy. He is Finn's father, after all.

Whichever way I turn, it's like I'm trapped . . .

He spent the next few hours trying to do some work on his computer, but found it impossible to concentrate. Impatient and frustrated, he flicked off the machine. He stood in the middle of the room, dipped his hand into his pocket.

The coins chinked. He remembered the damp beret lying on the pavement by the buskers' feet.

Heads . . . I say nothing to Jade.

Tails . . . I play the messenger.

He spun the silver coin into the air, suddenly reminded of the ghostly juggler, spinning his oranges.

He caught the coin and folded his hand over it . . .

He waited until he saw Jade pushing Finn back from nursery, then scooted across the road.

"Daniel!" Jade looked untidy and preoccupied. "I haven't seen you all weekend. Are you OK?"

He explained about Barnaby and spending time in Woodstock, looking after Laura. "She's heartbroken."

"I'm not surprised. Send her my love . . . and come in for a drink of something cool."

"Thanks." He hesitated. "I've got something else to tell you."

"Oh?" Jade looked at him more carefully. "Ah . . . I'll settle Finn, so we can talk."

"I was in Oxford this morning," Daniel said slowly.

They were in the garden, Finn digging in the sandpit, he and Jade sitting on the terrace. "On an errand in the Covered Market. I had a funny feeling I was being watched."

Jade groaned. "Don't tell me . . . Kieran."

"Yes. He ran up behind me in the Turl, blocked my path. I couldn't escape."

"I hope you told him to get lost."

"Not exactly."

Jade flushed. "But you *know* I don't want to see him. I've *told* you how I feel."

Daniel swallowed back a surge of impatience. "It was difficult. There was something very anxious about him . . . He says he only wants to talk. He says it's urgent, that he knows where you live."

She said grimly, "Yeah. He rang me . . . He came banging on the door."

"So you *have* seen him again! You might have told me!"

"No, I haven't seen him. Mum answered the door. I was out with Finn." Her voice rose. "How many more times must I tell you? I'm not seeing Kieran again. Not now. Not ever."

Daniel pushed his chair away from the terrace table. "There's no need to shout. This isn't my problem. I was in two minds about even passing on the message. But if you'll listen for two minutes together, here it is: Kieran wants you to meet him tonight, at six o'clock, outside Blackwell's."

Jade's voice was deadly calm. "Are you on his side?"

He leaned towards her and took her hand. "Of course not.

But maybe you should meet him, talk to him for half an hour. Listen to what he has to say. Get it over and done with."

"If you'd *any* idea how much he'd hurt me, you'd never even suggest—"

He slid his hand away and stood up. "Bloody hell, Jade . . . I'm *sick* of talking about Kieran. I just want him out of your life . . . And out of mine!"

"You and me both. But I'm not changing my mind."

"OK, I get the picture. The answer's no."

She looked up at him, her eyes dark with anger. "The answer's no."

"And I suppose you want me to meet him and tell him you're not coming? I'm not your pet slave, you know, running around Oxford for you on another errand."

Jade shook her head. "I'm not asking you to. Ignore him. Treat him as if he doesn't exist, just like he treated me."

Finn raced towards her. She caught the child in her arms, lifted him onto her lap.

Daniel looked down at the way their bodies twined around each other. He remembered Gran sitting on the terrace, her head nodding over a novel, her gnarled hands clutching at the book as it slipped away from her.

"Built a castle, Dan." Finn waved a sandy fist at him. "Come and see."

"Not now, Finn." Suddenly the only thing he wanted to do was to lie down and sleep for a week. "Not right now."

"Another time, hey?" Jade's mouth twitched into a half-smile that did not reach her eyes.

"Sure." Daniel turned to leave. "Another time."

He waited until the last moment before he decided.

He stood in the kitchen with Clare, laying the table for supper. He looked at his watch. Ten minutes to six. If he cycled like hell, he might just make it. He flung down the knives and forks, and bolted for the door.

I can't leave Kieran hanging about in town. He might go straight to Jade's again, make everything worse. I'll have to tell him I tried.

"Where are you going?" Clare called.

"Just remembered something I have to do . . . Back as soon as I can."

Kieran paced up and down outside Blackwell's, his face pale.

He'd changed his clothes since this morning. Now he wore a white shirt with a short black waistcoat and tight black jeans. A crisp red scarf fluttered at his neck. His hair gleamed in its ponytail.

Daniel cycled towards him.

"You're late. Where's Jade?" Kieran's eyes narrowed with anger. "Didn't you give her my message?"

"Yes, I did." Daniel got off the bike, but kept the machine between them. It felt safer that way. "She doesn't want to know. OK?"

Kieran moved closer and grabbed his shoulder. "You're *sure* you tried?"

Daniel shook himself free. Kieran's breath stank of tobacco. The anger bubbled up again. "Quite sure . . . and frankly, I'm sick of being your stupid little go-between. She won't see you and the matter's closed."

"Ooh, the matter's closed," Kieran mimicked. "This isn't a school debate on the environment. You're a bit of a pompous twit, aren't you?"

"Now look here—"

"No, *you* look here." Kieran flushed with rage. "I saw the wee child in Jade's arms —" he was watching Daniel carefully for his reaction — "and it's because of him I have to see her." He took a deep breath. "I don't mean I'd like to or want to. I'm not trying to organise a posh Oxford party on the river. *I mean I have to.* Can you get that into your head?"

"No." Daniel's anger had worn itself out. Weariness and

hunger engulfed him. "Your fight's with Jade, not with me. Sort it between you. From now on, leave me out of it."

"So the child *is* mine?" Kieran asked the question fast, as if he'd been storing ammunition and now fired it between Daniel's eyes.

It caught him unawares. "Finn," Daniel said carefully, his voice deadpan, as if he were reciting a text, "is Jade's little brother. He's not your flesh and blood. Now, if you *don't* mind—"

"You're *lying*."

"Look, this is ridiculous. First you accuse me of—"

"Finn's his name, is it?"

Shit. It slipped out. I shouldn't have told him. "It might be."

"It's a glorious Irish name. She's called him after me. The child's my double. I nearly died of shock when I saw him. I had absolutely no idea—"

Daniel's remaining patience evaporated.

"I've had enough of this." He flung a leg over his bike, gripped the handlebars and gritted his teeth. "Do us all a big favour and fuck off."

He spun the front wheel away from Kieran and pushed swiftly away.

Keiran's voice behind him came quiet and deadly.

"All right then, leave, why don't you? But you haven't won

this battle. Not by a long chalk. I need to talk to Jade, come hell or high water. And by God I will!"

His voice rose as Daniel cycled off.

"Don't say you haven't been warned."

I was watching at the window.

I saw Daniel cycle off – and I stood there until I saw him come back. I wanted to run out after him, ask him if he'd seen Kieran.

Then I decided I didn't want to know whether he had or not.

I knew I wasn't being fair to Daniel, getting him involved in all this. As he said, it's not his problem. It's just that I like him a lot. I can talk to him. And I trust him. I've never felt that way about anyone – least of all Kieran.

With Kieran, I was always trying to prove something. With Daniel, I can be myself. There's all the difference in the world.

I went downstairs. I told Mum that Kieran had been pestering Daniel. She said look, maybe the situation was getting more serious. Maybe we should go to the police, tell them that Kieran was beginning to harass us.

I said no way. I didn't want to get the police involved, asking all kinds of personal questions. There's no knowing what Kieran might be capable of if he thought we'd ratted on him.

So then Mum said, "Look, Jay, I'm still not happy about all this. OK, we don't have to go to the police. But what about a bit of discreet legal advice?"

I said, "But nothing *serious* has actually happened."

"That's precisely my point. If we take proper legal advice now, maybe we can prevent the worst – whatever that might be. Talking to a family lawyer could only help. I know someone in London. He's got years of experience in dealing with all kinds of complicated family matters. Why don't I give him a ring, make an appointment to see him?"

"Like when?"

"I think it should be as soon as possible. Let's take the bull by the horns. What about tomorrow, if he can fit us in?"

At first I said no. I couldn't face having to talk to an outsider about Finn, going over the whole story again. It's painful, all this remembering. As far as I'm concerned, the fewer people who know the truth the better.

I went out to the garden, sat on Finn's swing to have a think.

But Mum followed me out, stuck to her guns. Said she thought the meeting would only help, and could she ring Stuart straight away, see whether tomorrow would be possible?

I said, "You're making a mountain out of a molehill."

"Rubbish. It's a question of protecting Finn. And he's worth protecting, isn't he?"

"You know I'd kill for him."

"There." Mum gave me a kiss. "That's what I wanted to hear . . . I'm going straight in to ring Stuart."

After she'd left, the garden felt empty and lonely. Finn's toys littered the lawn. His little castle still stood, a bit wonky, in the sandpit.

I gave him life, didn't I?

So spending a couple of unpleasant hours talking about him to a lawyer, coming clean about my being his mum and wanting to make sure he could stay with me safe and sound – suddenly that seemed like a small price to pay.

It felt like the very least I could do.

Daniel

He was still chomping through a piece of burnt breakfast toast when the doorbell rang.

Jade said, "Hi. I wanted to say sorry."

He swallowed some dry crumbs. "Whatever for?"

"For being so bad-tempered yesterday."

"You weren't. Don't be an idiot."

"It's just that even the name Kieran makes me want to throw things at the cat!"

He grinned. "Then it's a good job you haven't got one!" He looked her up and down. "You're extremely well ironed today."

Jade laughed. "You mean that usually I'm not! Well, today I've made a special effort. Mum and I have to go to London. We've an appointment with someone this afternoon. We didn't know about it until last night."

Wait for it. I'm going to get involved again.

Jade chuntered on. "I've come to ask you a big favour. A huge one. More important than anything to do with Kieran."

His heart sank a fraction. "Ask away."

"Could you collect Finn from the nursery for me? We're

going to London by car – Mum hates trains – and you know what the traffic can be like. I wouldn't ask if I didn't trust you with my life."

"Sure, no problem. What time does he—"

"Three o'clock. The nursery's on the Banbury Road." She grabbed his right hand and turned it over. A frisson of excitement surged through him. "Here, I'll write the number on your wrist." She pulled a biro from her pocket, scrawling three digits onto his skin. "I'm going to drop Finn there now. I'll let the teachers know you'll be collecting him."

He crushed a sudden longing to touch her cheek, her forehead that puckered into furrows as she wrote. "What do you want me to do with him afterwards?"

"Take him back to ours . . . Here are the keys . . . The big brass one is for the front door."

"I know." He cradled the keys in his palm, bitterly remembering the moment when Martin told him the estate agent needed them. "These used to be mine."

"Of course." Jade looked shamefaced. "I'm so sorry . . . I keep forgetting."

"It's OK."

Jade rushed on, "Mum'll leave lots of stuff in the fridge for tea. Have whatever you fancy. Finn loves cheese and nuts and raisins. And biscuits. He'll tell you!"

"We'll have a great time."

"I'll explain all about it to him on the way to the nursery."

Jade reached up to Daniel and kissed him. He could smell her lemony fragrance.

"Thank you *so* much. We should be back well before six."

"Don't worry about a thing."

Jade walked down the path, looking subdued and determined. She waved and crossed the road.

Daniel said flatly, "Have a good day," and shut the door. He crushed the keys into his pocket, feeling the coolness of her lips on his.

He felt uneasy and restless.

Collecting Finn was an exciting prospect but also surprisingly daunting. Jade had paid him a huge compliment, putting her trust in him – but still, he couldn't help feeling a shade resentful. Was she beginning to make use of him?

To quash the unease, he flung himself into the day: mowing the lawn for Clare, cycling to the Summertown library, eating lunch without knowing what he put into his mouth. He kept checking his watch. He started to wonder who Jade and Eve had gone to see with such unplanned urgency – and whether it had anything to do with Kieran's abrupt appearance on the scene.

He replayed last night's meeting in his head. He shouldn't have sworn at Kieran. It might have made things worse. Kieran had threatened something, but nothing specific. He was probably all mouth. Anyway, Daniel told himself sternly for the umpteenth time, it really wasn't his problem. He should put the whole thing out of his head.

At a quarter to three, just as he was about to leave the house, the phone rang. Clare was out shopping. It was a message for Martin from one of his Oxfam colleagues overseas. The voice at the other end droned on while Daniel scribbled down the complicated details.

He checked the number on his wrist and the keys in his pocket. Then he rushed out for his bike, suddenly realising that he'd be wheeling Finn home in his pushchair and he couldn't possibly handle both.

He grabbed his skateboard: it'd be faster than running, and once he was at the nursery he could tuck it under one arm and still manage Finn.

He began zooming down Chalfont Road. Into the stifling afternoon heat, a faint mizzle of rain had begun to fall, coating the pavements with a treacly sheen.

He reached the Woodstock Road, waited impatiently for a gap in the traffic, raced across the road and mounted his skateboard again. He checked his watch. It was already three o'clock and he still hadn't reached the Banbury Road.

Panic made his mouth dry and his heart thump against his ribs.

Come on! I should be there by now, waiting for Finn with all the parents. Odd one out . . .

He bent his head against the rain, concentrating on the speed of the skateboard beneath his feet, the trundling hum of its wheels as he crashed his way down Staverton Road. He reached the corner of the Banbury Road and without looking or thinking, zipped around it.

A young mother walked towards him, holding the hand of a toddler in a pink frock. The child was looking up into her mum's face, grumbling about the rain, asking to be picked up. Neither of them noticed Daniel until it was almost too late.

He swerved to avoid them, crashed into a low brick wall, and fell heavily across the pavement. The skateboard zoomed into the road. A car screeched to a halt. Daniel lay, his head thundering, his right ankle burning and twisted. Patches of sky, trees, busy road, wet pavement and a small child's face swam across his vision, blurred and muddled.

For a moment the world spun cloudy and grey.

"Are you all right?"

He struggled to sit up. A sharp pain shot from his ankle to his thigh. His head felt as if a giant had used it as a battering ram. "I'm OK . . . thanks."

The child's mother bent towards him. "Here's your skate-board. The car managed to stop in time . . . Thank God you skidded towards the wall and not into the road!"

"Yes." He clawed at the bricks and stood up. The pavement swayed. He blinked. The bright fuchsia pink of the child's frock hurt his eyes. "I'm late . . . I've got to go . . . to find –" he squinted at the number on his wrist – "number 141."

"You want the nursery? We've just come from there." She tucked the skateboard under his arm. "I always thought these were lethal."

"Which way is it?" Daniel asked wildly.

"That way." She pointed towards town, then looked at him anxiously. "But I'd walk if I were you."

"Or hobble," he muttered sourly.

47, 63, 71, 89, 103, 131 . . . God, I'm such an idiot.

He checked his watch.

And now it's a quarter past three . . .

I can't walk any faster . . . My ankle hurts like hell . . .

*

THE ROSEGARDEN NURSERY said the sign.

Tied to the post were three canary-yellow balloons. As Daniel limped past, loose pebbles splayed out from beneath his feet. One of the balloons burst with a crack of gunfire.

He crashed on the door, was surprised to find it open and pushed against it. He stepped gingerly into a tiled hall. It smelt of detergent and chocolate.

There was nobody about. A row of low pegs lined the wall. Several still held small sweaters. On one dangled a tiny pair of trainers, on another a white cotton hat. Voices laughed and children chattered to each other from behind a door.

Phew! I'm not the last . . .

He knocked at the door.

"Please come in!"

He turned the handle. A long room lay in front of him, its wooden floor polished and gleaming. A man on his hands and knees packed coloured bricks and soft toys into an enormous trunk. A pair of young twins, identically dressed, played by the window.

"Hi," a girl with flat blonde hair called from behind the piano. "Can I help?"

"I've come for Finn Davenport." Daniel's voice seemed to echo to the ceiling.

The girl stood up. "Finn's already gone."

Daniel's hands pricked with pins and needles. "He can't have."

"He went on the dot of three o'clock."

"Who collected him? Was it his sister?"

"No, his dad . . . Tall man, dark hair. Looked the spitting image of Finn . . . His sister, Jade, she told me this morning that someone called Daniel would be fetching him."

Daniel closed his eyes.

This can't be happening. Tell me this is a nightmare and any minute I'll wake up.

He said, "But that's me. *I'm* Daniel. You've let Finn go off with the wrong guy."

The girl frowned. She walked swiftly towards him. "I don't understand. Finn must be with his father, they looked so alike. So what's the problem?"

Daniel groaned. "I can't explain . . . You shouldn't have done it, that's all."

The girl flushed. "Look, I'm sorry. But there were crowds of parents at the door, everyone milling around . . . How was I to know?"

He tried to collect his scattered wits. "You weren't . . . It's OK." He felt numb with shock, completely unsure what he was going to do. "I don't suppose you happened to see whether Finn's father had a car?"

"I'm sorry, I've no idea." She sprinted to the door and glanced into the hall. "Finn's pushchair's disappeared, so he must have been taken home in that."

"Right."

Daniel stood as if rooted to the spot. He realised what a mess he must look: his jeans grimy with mud and rain, the skateboard bent, his hair wild. The twins had stopped playing. They were staring at him, their mouths open, their round eyes dark as raisins. The piano seemed to be floating several inches above the floor.

The man filling the trunk waved a toy at him. A bear with a grey face and one eye gazed anxiously at Daniel.

"Doesn't this belong to Finn? He must've forgotten to take it home with him."

Daniel clutched Harriet's stiff, furry limbs with his free hand.

"Yes," he said. "She does."

His body came to life.

Ignoring the shriek of pain in his ankle, he started to run.

Away from the room, through the hall, out of the door, down the garden, into the relentless thrum of traffic on the Banbury Road.

Jade

I had a totally crap day.

First I felt carsick. It was partly nerves, trying to gear myself up to talking to a total stranger about my private life. Then there was an accident on the motorway and the traffic ground to a halt. It took us three and a half hours to get into the centre of London. Mum and I drank our bottle of water in the first hour, and crawling along like a tortoise in a thunderstorm was frustrating as hell.

I started to fret about Finn, whether Daniel would be able to cope.

Mum said, "Stop being such a worry-guts, Jay. Daniel's one of the nicest, most capable young men I've ever met."

"Yeah, I like him a lot."

"Well, then, leave him to it. He's spent loads of time with Finn, it's not like they're strangers—"

"But Finn can be a handful. He knows all the tricks of the trade. And he's never had Daniel on his own before."

"So let Daniel work out how to handle him." She glanced at me and smiled. "It'll be good experience for him!"

*

Eventually we reached the Strand.

Mum managed to find a parking space and we had a sandwich lunch. We crossed a filthy street to Stuart's offices, cranked up to the fifth floor in a lift that smelled of yesterday's food.

I haven't been to London for years. It doesn't get any cleaner, that's for sure.

Stuart was polite and aloof in a horrible, snooty kind of way. When we shook hands, his was cold and slimy. I could feel him looking at me, sizing me up, as if his eyes were cameras.

Then we sat down and the questions began. When and where had I met Kieran, how long had I known him, how old was Finn? He took notes in amazingly fast shorthand, kept peering at me over his rimless spectacles. I felt distinctly grubby and uncomfortable, like I was confessing a sordid "Pregnant at Thirteen!" story for the tabloids.

I felt more and more depressed. Yes, I'd had a crush on a teacher. But I had to take it further, didn't I? I wasn't happy until I'd taken things all the way . . . *He* should've known better. But the way Stuart kept looking at me, I could practically hear him thinking that the person who should've known better was *me* . . .

But instead of coming out with it – "You *have* got yourself into a stupid mess, haven't you, Miss Davenport?" — there was a lot of legal language about parental rights, access, injunctions, mumbo-jumbo stuff. Stuart and Mum began to talk details, like I wasn't sitting beside them at all, like I simply wasn't there.

I switched off.

I started staring out of the grimy window at the landscape of rooftops and a mangy-looking cat draping himself around a chimney-pot. I thought how wonderful it would be to have no responsibilities, just like the cat. All he has to do each day is to find a decent meal and sleep in the sun.

All *I* wanted was to get shot of Kieran for ever.

To be back in Oxford, in the garden, playing with Finn.

With Daniel beside me.

I could hardly wait to get home.

Laura

I waited until four o'clock and then I rang the boy.

For some reason, I'd been thinking about him all afternoon. I felt in my bones that something was wrong, like that really bad feeling you get when you wake up after a nightmare and all day you can't shake off that dark, evil shadow.

It was worse than wrong.

When he answered the phone, he sounded hysterical.

At first he didn't make any sense at all. Said he was supposed to be at Jade's, he'd only hobbled back to Clare and Martin's to see if there'd been any messages. Said he had to search Oxford. Except he didn't know where to start looking.

I didn't have a clue what he was on about. I said calm down, take a deep breath, talk to me slowly. I was frantic with worry, but I tried not to let him hear it.

He said, "Finn's been kidnapped. From his nursery school. Jade asked me to collect him. I had a bit of an accident on my skateboard. I was only a few minutes late. I've let her down so badly."

I said, "But who on earth would have taken him? And why?"

And the story about Finn's father came pouring out.

I said, didn't Jade know where Kieran lived? Where he might have taken Finn? The boy said, no, it could be anywhere, he'd tried to find out, but Jade didn't *want* to know. She'd been devastated to see Kieran in Oxford and refused to have anything to do with him.

Then the boy started crying.

He said, "If anything serious has happened to Finn, I'll never forgive myself, Jade'll never forgive me, my life won't be worth living."

I told him the situation wasn't his fault, he'd simply been caught up in it. He must keep his nerve, sit down, think everything out as calmly as he could.

He said he was sorry to make such a fuss, but he had to go.

I said, "Ring me later, tonight, as soon as you've any news."

He said he'd try.

I put down the phone and my heart went out to him.

Daniel

This is a complete and utter nightmare.

Any minute now, I'll wake up and everything will be back to normal.

But it wasn't.

Anything but.

He'd limped back to Clare and Martin's to dump the skateboard, check for messages. Then he'd leaped to answer the phone. For a wild moment he hoped it might be Kieran ringing to apologise, explain, arrange a sensible meeting . . .

Fat chance.

Talking to Laura calmed him down a bit, but not for long.

He dried his eyes, crashed down to the kitchen for a glass of water, tried to smooth his hair. He grabbed a pot of honey from the shelf, swallowed a huge dollop and flung the sticky spoon into the sink, wishing he could hurl Kieran down the drain.

His head throbbed and the pain in his ankle nagged. He wanted to get out of the house before Clare returned. He couldn't face having to explain everything to her. He might have to later. But not now. She didn't know the truth about Finn – and he'd no right to tell her without Jade's permission.

He dragged himself over the road, let himself into Jade's house and slammed the door.

Gran! I wish you were here! I could really do with your help right now . . .

The silence drummed in his ears.

He checked the answerphone in the hall. The red light shone steadily back at him, a cruel unblinking eye. Nothing. No messages.

He drooped his way into the kitchen, slumped at the table, his head in his hands.

"Don't say you haven't been warned . . ."

He hadn't guessed what Kieran was planning. That Finn would be involved. He'd assumed Kieran was only after Jade.

How stupid could you get?

He should have worked it out, told Jade immediately. Maybe he could have prevented the kidnap.

Except you can't put a police cordon round a child before anything has happened to him. You can't keep watch twenty-four seven. Sooner or later, if that's what Kieran was mad enough to plot, he'd have found a hairline crack in the armour, a sliver of a moment.

That was all it took.

Kieran must've been watching this house. He must've seen Jade talking to me, taking Finn to school, driving off with Eve. How else could he have known the coast might be clear? He's a nutter. Hasn't he got anything better to do?

Daniel shivered.

If I'd got to the nursery fifteen minutes earlier, maybe I'd have frightened Kieran away. He'd have seen me and decided not to risk it. As it was, I played straight into his hands.

And Finn . . . He knew I'd be collecting him. I wonder how Kieran managed to persuade him to go with him without a fuss . . . Maybe Kieran had a pocketful of sweets or a new teddy bear.

Jade will never forgive me . . . Nor Eve . . .

Where are *they? I haven't got a number, I can't even ring them . . .*

Should I ring the police?

Maybe it's still a bit soon . . . How do you judge something like this? . . . And would Jade want *me to? I can't take that decision on my own.*

There's nothing I can do but wait.

For twenty minutes he sat in the kitchen, waiting for the front door to open, the phone to ring – anything that might spell Jade's return or a message from Kieran.

When the fridge buzzed into life, his heart thumped with alarm. A sparrow crashed against the window-pane. Daniel jumped as if he'd been shot.

He longed to hear Finn's endless babble of questions, his squeals of laughter and delight.

"'Lo, Dan . . . Made a castle . . . Come and see."

In the distance a siren wailed. Daniel's mouth tasted sour and revolting.

He paced up and down the hall, peered through the window into the road, checked the phone was working. He dialled the operator, asked whether she had a number for a Kieran McVeigh in Oxford, amazed he hadn't thought of doing it sooner.

No, there was nothing listed.

I can't bear this waiting a minute longer. I'm going to cycle into Oxford, see whether the musicians are busking. Kieran might be there. I've got to try. They might be playing without him. One of the violinists might give me his address.

He limped over the road for his bike, pedalled as fast as he could into St Giles. Wheeling his bike and leaning on it for support, he walked into Cornmarket.

The ghost on stilts cackled with glee.

Daniel stared into the shadowy lunatic eyes.

They blinked.

A battered orange rolled towards his feet.

I couldn't believe what I heard.

I mean, I couldn't take it in. Daniel stood at our front door, his face all white and peaky, holding Harriet and saying, "I don't know how to tell you."

"What?" I said. "Tell me what? Where's Finn?"

"He's disappeared. He was collected from the nursery before I got there. By someone else." His voice choked. "It must've been Kieran. The girl at the nursery said Kieran looked so like Finn that she assumed he was his father and didn't give it a second thought."

"But I told her that Daniel would be—"

"She didn't think to check his name. And anyway, even if she had, Kieran would've bluffed it somehow. He must've been set on getting Finn out of the way as fast as he could . . . I'm so sorry . . . I was only a few minutes late."

"A few *minutes*?"

"I was on my skateboard, going as fast as I could. I swerved to avoid a kid and her mother and I fell off. I hurt my head and my ankle . . . I swear it was only a few—"

"Do you expect me to believe that? I mean, what *else* have

you been doing this afternoon? Wasn't collecting Finn your top priority? I ask you to do the simplest thing for me, the easiest, most straightforward chore in the world, and you can't even get *that* right. You *knew* how important this was."

"Please, Jade, you can't know how sorry I—"

"I'll *never* forgive you – and I'll never, ever, trust you again."

Mum stepped in. "Don't be absurd, Jay. This isn't Daniel's fault, there's no point lashing out at him. This is entirely Kieran's madness. What on earth could he *want* with Finn?"

Then Daniel turned on me.

"This is all *your* fault," he said. "If you'd agreed to meet Kieran and talk to him, like I asked you to, none of this would have happened."

My fault!

I lost it completely. Without thinking, I slapped Daniel across the face. *Wham!* It stung my hand, so it must've really hurt him. His eyes went all startled and he put his hand to his cheek as if he couldn't believe what I'd done.

Mum said, "Calm down, both of you. Jay, apologise to Daniel at once. And stop playing this pointless blame game. If we haven't heard from Kieran by seven o'clock, I'm ringing the police."

"Oh, no, you're not," I shouted. "I don't want the police

involved, this is nothing to do with them. This is *my* problem and I'm going to solve it. I've had quite enough of spilling the beans for one day. I'm not answering any more questions from anybody."

Mum went ballistic. I've never seen her hit the roof like that before.

"You're behaving like a spoilt bloody brat," she yelled. "I've supported you 100 per cent, right down the line, up until today, but now I couldn't be more ashamed of you. It's not a question of 'spilling the beans'. I'll tell the police that Finn's *my* son, that *I'm* responsible, that I've got no idea who might have kidnapped the child. I'm willing to go on covering up for you, but I only hope you understand the strain it puts on me. Why can't you *grow up?*"

She hurled her bag across the hall and vanished into the kitchen. I could hear her crashing the cups around.

My legs were shaking. I sat down on the stairs. Inside my head, I was shouting *Finn, where are you? Are you in danger? Don't worry, sweetheart. We'll come and find you.*

Everything went black, like in the garden when Daniel guessed the truth.

He came and sat down beside me. He put his arms round me. I could feel the warmth of his body, all sturdy and comforting.

I clung to him. I wouldn't let myself cry.

I said, "I'm sorry I hit you. I didn't mean to . . . And I'm sorry I shouted . . . But Jesus, Daniel, what the hell are we going to do?"

"Kieran's trying to blackmail you." He stroked my hair. "To get Finn back, you'll *have* to see Kieran, you'll have to talk to him."

"What a bastard . . . What kind of a man could behave like this?"

"We know what kind of man he is. Last night, when I told him you'd refused to see him, he yelled, *'Don't say you haven't been warned.'* But I never imagined he'd do anything like this."

Mum called us from the kitchen, saying she'd made us a cup of tea.

I kept thinking, *I'm living in a nightmare.*

I haven't spent a night without Finn since he was born.

I can't sleep a wink until I know he's safe and sound.

Damn Kieran. Damn him to hell.

Where is he now?

Where has he taken my son?

And why?

After all this time, what can Kieran possibly want with me?

Daniel

At seven o'clock Eve said quietly, "Jay, go upstairs and tidy yourself up. I'm ringing the police."

Jade flung herself out of the room.

Eve turned to Daniel. "I'd like you to go."

He gaped at her. "But I can't *leave* you like this."

"Yes, you can." She took his arm, marched him into the hall. "I must ring Bobby. He's so busy at the moment that I dread disturbing him, but he's got to know about Finn. Then I'll ring the police."

"But I need to talk to them, tell them what happened."

"No. It's kind of you to offer, but I don't want you to be involved. At least, no more than you already are."

"But—"

"Don't argue, Daniel. None of this is your problem. We'll tell the police Finn was abducted from the nursery. They may want to interview the staff. The fact that *you'd* been trying to collect him is neither here nor there."

"But I'm *responsible*—"

"*No, you are not.*" Eve lowered her voice. "We asked you to help us out and you did your best. You didn't plan to fall off your skateboard at the last moment. Anyway, this whole affair is *Jade's* responsibility. The sooner she admits it, the better."

Eve opened the front door. The rain had stopped, but it hadn't cleared the air. The stale heat of early evening wafted in to them.

He said desperately, "I'm sorry, Eve. I'm not going anywhere until I've told the police what happened. It'll only take five minutes. I'll tell them why I was late, what the nursery said to me. Then I'll go back to Clare and Martin's . . . OK?"

Eve sighed. "OK," she said. "I'm too tired to fight. You win."

Martin said, "There's a police car over the road, outside the Davenports."

Daniel stared blindly at a pathetic quiz game on TV.

"Danny?" Martin stuffed his pipe with tobacco. "Is anything wrong?"

Canned laughter burbled from the screen. "Who with?"

"You're not listening to me." Martin struck a match, sucked at the pipe's stem. "With the Davenports."

Daniel stuffed another toffee in his mouth. "How would I know?"

"Well, you're great friends with them, aren't you? Thought you might know."

"Haven't a clue." He pulled himself out of his chair. "Got a bit of a headache, Martin. Fell off my skateboard this afternoon . . . I'm going to bed."

A haze of blue pipe smoke filtered across the room.

"Sorry to hear that, Danny. I'll ask Clare to pop up later, make sure you're OK."

He stood by the window, watching, fretting, limping up and down, imagining the questions Jade and Eve would be facing.

He'd answered the questions the police had fired at him, then been asked to leave.

Miserably, he'd gone back to Clare and Martin's.

The police car sat outside for more than an hour. Then in an instant it sped away.

Where's Finn now? Asleep in the back of a car, being driven God knows where? Maybe even on a plane? In tears, screaming for his mum?

He stripped off his clothes, slid into bed. When Clare tapped at his door and pushed it open, he pretended to be asleep.

Later, he fell into a fitful doze, his ears straining for the sound of a car stopping across the road, anything that might spell an end to the agony of waiting.

A storm began to brew in the distance. Intermittent cracks of lightning splintered across the sky. He pattered to the curtains and peered out at Jade's. Lights shone from every window.

The hands of his clock ticked together at midnight.

The storm drew closer. Grumbles of thunder followed the lightning. Rain began to splatter in handfuls against the window-pane.

He flung back the bedclothes, pulled on his dressing-gown and opened his door.

Clare and Martin must be sound asleep by now.

He tiptoed down to the hall and picked up the phone.

"Laura? Did I wake you?"

He heard her gasp of relief. "Absolutely not. I've been waiting for you to ring. Any news?"

"Nothing. We stuck it out until seven o'clock. Then Eve rang the police. I gave them my side of the story and then I came back here. I've got this terrible feeling I could've prevented the whole thing." His voice choked. "They're going to keep up the story—"

"That Finn is Eve's child?"

"Yeah . . . God, Laura, I feel so *useless*—"

"Listen . . . I know someone who might be able to help."

"What d'you mean?"

"It's a long story. Too long for this hour of the night – and not for the telephone."

"So how—"

"I'll drive over to yours first thing tomorrow morning."

"OK. If you think it'll help."

"It's better than doing nothing."

Daniel agreed. "Anything's better than that!"

"One other thing."

"Yes?"

"We'll need photos of Finn and Jade – and something that belongs to him. Have you got anything? A scarf, some clothes, an old toy?"

Daniel shivered. He glanced round the dark hall with its spooky shadows. A stroke of lightning lit the floor, shimmered it pale blue. The colour of Kieran's eyes.

He said slowly, "Whatever for?"

"I'll explain tomorrow. Good night, Daniel. Try to get some sleep."

After I'd rung the boy at four o'clock, I couldn't settle to anything.

I walked for a bit in Blenheim, to clear my head, but it's not the same without the blithering pooch. Then I went home, made a vain attempt to check some notes, but I couldn't concentrate. I kept thinking if only there was *something* I could do.

Then I remembered. Sylvia. Her voice, her presence, shimmered into my mind.

I first met her, oh, it must be ten years ago. Daddy and I were asked to this posh party at Trinity College. Big affair, hundreds of people milling about. Daddy was dragged off to meet some famous visiting professor the other side of the room.

I was standing there on my own when I became aware that someone was at my elbow, examining me closely, almost inspecting for flaws! And a deep, gutteral voice said, "You are looking for someone you have lost."

I turned round and said laughingly, "Not really. My father's always in demand," but then I stared at this woman and I knew immediately she wasn't talking about Daddy.

She was tall and stately, wearing a long midnight-blue dress. She had a mass of stark-white hair, dark eyebrows like crescent moons and the deepest pitch-black eyes I'd ever seen. They looked through me and through me again.

She said, "Ah, this is not your father. It is someone else entirely."

I must have gone yellow with shock. I said, "But nobody else knows about her. How do *you*?"

"Because you carry her around with you. She is a part of your life, of your very being, whether you realise it or not."

And then she turned away.

Afterwards, I found out who she was. A famous psychic called Sylvia, they told me, with quite extraordinary powers. I asked for her address. She lived in Eastleach Turville, a tiny village near Cirencester. I filed the information in my head.

A week later, I made sure Daddy had left the cottage. I rang Sylvia and she agreed to see me.

I told her the little I knew. I had nothing to give her, no photographs. My only meagre information was a date and place of birth. Sylvia sat holding my hand for a long time. She said she felt *she* was alive and safe. She couldn't hear her voice, no special messages were coming through.

And she couldn't tell me any more.

I started to cry. I remember that vividly. It was the first time I'd ever cried, to hear *her* being spoken about.

Daddy and I — we never talked about her. Like it was an unspoken agreement, we pretended she didn't exist.

Several months later, I read about Sylvia in a Sunday magazine interview. The reporter said how sceptical he'd been about people with psychic powers, how he thought crystal balls and star signs were a load of daft mumbo-jumbo.

But then he'd met Sylvia. She'd told him stuff about his life nobody else on earth could possibly have known. He described how on three separate cases, the police had asked for her help. She'd given them details that led them straight to the right spot.

So after the boy rang me at midnight, I got on the phone. Sylvia said yes, she could see us in the morning. I told her how grateful I was, I'd pay her anything she asked.

She said that was fine.

But she'd prefer to meet with Daniel on his own . . .

After Daniel had gone, Mum took the brunt of the questions the police asked us.

I sat there pretending to be an obedient daughter, a good older sister, while everyone treated me like a silly little girl. Oh dear, how very careless of me to lose my brother! Was I sure he'd reached the nursery safely this morning? Yes, of course I was. Had I given any different instructions to the staff? Yes, that Daniel would be collecting Finn. The staff would have to be interviewed, of course. Could we think of any reason why Finn had been snatched?

Both Mum and I went very quiet at that point.

Mum battled on, but I could sense that the police — we had one man and one woman — felt we weren't telling them the whole truth. They asked us how long we'd lived here, where we'd lived before, why we'd moved to Oxford, where was Dad? It's like your entire life is under the microscope. It makes you *feel* guilty, whether you've done anything wrong or not.

I'll never forgive Kieran for this.

The police told us not to worry, they'd "put all the wheels

in motion". They were very sympathetic. They gave us the names of helplines and counsellors we could contact if we needed to.

Inside me, my heart was screaming for help, begging for Finn's return.

I gave them a photo of me and Finn in the garden, playing on the swing. I told them what he'd been wearing this morning, down to the make of his shoes. I said, "He's got different colour eyes. One's a deep blue, the other's speckled with green."

I wanted to say, "And he's mine. He's my little boy. If you can't see that, you must be blind."

They said they'd "be in touch". At the door, just when I thought we'd finally got rid of them, they asked Mum whether she'd be willing to make a TV appeal.

If they didn't have any news by tomorrow.

Mum was rattled and exhausted, but she said, "Of course. If you think it might help. My husband's flying home tomorrow on the first plane he can get. He'll come with us. Just let us know what we need to do."

I went up to Finn's room. I didn't want Mum to see me crying. She looked whacked. Said she'd make us something to eat, we had to keep our strength up, it was probably going to be the longest night of our lives.

I stood at Finn's window. I looked out at the garden, at Finn's sandpit, his toys all over the grass. I'd left them there for him and Daniel to play with. I looked down to his swing, hanging limp and empty.

I thought, *What if he never climbs on it again?*

I must do something . . .

Anything . . .

I'll do anything it takes to get him back.

Daniel

He hung on to Jade's doorbell.

Eve answered it at once. "No news," she said. "But thanks for asking."

"How's Jade?"

"Mercifully still asleep . . . She was walking around the house like a ghost until the early hours."

He took a deep breath. "I want to try going from door to door, in the neighbourhood, asking whether anyone's seen Finn. I can't just sit doing nothing."

"If you think it'll do any good."

"It can't do any harm . . . The thing is, I need a photo, something that might jog people's memory."

"Of course." Eve went through to the living-room. The photograph album lay on the coffee table. "We gave the police one of Jade and Finn last night . . . Take your pick."

He leafed through the last few pages, extracted a photo of Finn that must have been taken several months ago in Brittany. "This'll be fine."

Harriet was lying on her back on the table.

"If you want to know what he was wearing yesterday —"
Eve's voice shook — "it was blue denim shorts, a red and
white striped T-shirt, red socks and white shoes." She
slumped into a chair. "Good luck."

"I haven't said anything yet to Clare and Martin. But if
there's any news—"

"Of course. Jade will ring you."

"Tell her I'm thinking of her all the time."

"I know, Daniel. Thanks."

The phone rang. Eve raced to answer it.

Behind her back, Daniel picked up Harriet. He stuffed the
bear into his pocket and slunk out of the house.

The moment he saw Laura's car pull up outside, he slammed
the front door behind him.

"Daniel! Did you get any sleep?"

"I crashed out after I spoke to you. I couldn't keep my eyes
open. Then I woke up at six, spark awake, feeling all guilty
and horrible."

"Has there been any—"

"Nothing. I've just been over to Jade's. Eve gave me a
photo of Finn." He dug a hand into his bag and pulled it out.
"And I've brought the photo of me and Jade at the school
dance. I didn't want to leave it behind, dangling from my

pinboard . . . And I've brought Harriet." His voice choked. "Finn left her at the nursery."

"He brought her to mine, that day they came to lunch." She revved the engine and drove to the top of Chalfont Road. The car still smelled of Barnaby.

"Where are we going, Laura?"

"To a tiny village in Gloucestershire, near Cirencester. It's divinely beautiful."

"But why do I need all this stuff?"

"Because I know this very special woman. Her name's Sylvia. She's a psychic."

His mouth tasted sour. "We're not getting into witchcraft, are we?"

Laura touched his hand. "She's not a witch, but she *has* got extraordinary powers. Her grandmother was a Romany gypsy. Sylvia's inherited her gift. You either have it or you don't."

"And Sylvia has it?"

"In spades. She practises psychometry. She takes something that belongs to a person and feels something, sees things, from it. That's why she'll need Harriet."

Laura slowed at the roundabout on Woodstock Road. "We'll follow the road to Burford, then turn left instead of right."

"Have you met her?"

Laura said quietly, "Once or twice. She's genuine, Daniel. She's not a freak. I wouldn't be taking you to see her if she were."

He was silent for a moment. Then he said, "The person who *should* be seeing her is Jade."

"I know." Laura glanced at him. "But if Sylvia has bad news, maybe it's better for us to see her first?"

"You mean, we can act as a kind of filter?"

"Exactly. Except there's no 'we' about it. Sylvia said she'd prefer to see you on your own."

"I'll be terrified."

"There's no need, I promise you . . . Let's hope she'll give you good news."

Daniel said bitterly, "I'm not holding my breath."

He stared out at the gentle Oxfordshire fields, some clipped and harvested, freshened from last night's rain, now basking underneath their August sun.

Everything looks so normal, so ordinary. I wonder where Finn has woken up this morning. Whose eyes is he looking into right now? Who is he talking to?

They sped past the sign to the Blue Cross sanctuary.

I'd been planning to buy Laura a puppy before Kieran erupted into my life . . . It's like now I've forgotten everything but finding Finn.

They turned left at the roundabout to Burford, drove on, then turned right, past the Cotswold Wildlife Park and up a winding, single-track path. Trees, heavy with late summer leaf, meshed branches overhead as if linking their hands in love. Fields stretched their shoulders into the clarity of sky.

The track narrowed even further. The car bumped and grumbled over the stones.

"Where are we now?" Daniel's heart began to thump with nerves.

"Once we get through these woods, we're nearly there."

A graceful valley swooped ahead of them: a bridge drifted over a meandering stream; an ancient church, fortress-like, guarded its corner; a cluster of cottages dotted the side of the hill.

"Sylvia lives there, in that little group of alms houses." Laura parked the car. "Hers is the one at the end. Walk through the garden and down the side to the back of the house. She'll be waiting for you."

His teeth chattered with fright. "Come in with me."

Laura gripped his hand. "Go it alone. It'll be better that

way, clearer for Sylvia, more straightforward . . . It's *you* she wants to see."

He took a deep breath, swung his bag over his shoulder.

"Wish me luck."

He climbed out of the car.

The air smelled fresh and sweet, of cut grass, pine needles and summer rain.

He pushed against a wooden gate, climbed a stony path through the fir-trees, and walked past the side of the house, hearing the pebbles crunch beneath his feet. Through one of the windows he glimpsed a vivid face crowned with a mass of white hair.

He tapped at the wooden door.

It stood ajar, as if beckoning him in.

When I woke it was ten o'clock. I heard Dad at the front door and Mum saying, "Bobby, darling . . . Thank God you're home."

I couldn't believe I'd slept at all.

Of course there was no news. I could hear Mum and Dad talking in the kitchen. They'd have woken me if there was anything to say.

I took a shower and tried to get my head together. I didn't have the strength to open Finn's door. Going into his room would have finished me off for the entire day. I walked past it quickly, looking the other way.

Dad was great. He gave me an enormous hug and said he was so pleased to be home with us. He could stay for a whole week and to hell with work. He said we were bound to find Finn, it was only a matter of time.

Mum rang the police. She spoke to the policewoman we saw last night. She said they hadn't picked up any clues yet and they thought talking to the press and making a TV appeal might be very useful.

Mum put the phone down and came back to the kitchen to tell us.

And suddenly I heard myself saying, quietly and calmly, "*I'm* going to do this. *I* want to make the appeal. I'm sick of pretending Finn's not my baby. I want everyone to know that he is."

Mum went a bit pale. She grabbed Dad's hand and I saw how their fingers locked together, white and frightened.

Dad said, "Are you absolutely sure you want to do this, Jay? Once you've done it, there'll be no going back."

I said, "I've spent all night thinking and deciding. I can't let Mum take the responsibility for this a minute longer. She's been lying for me. I want to tell the police the truth. And I want to do it right now, while I have the courage."

"Well, if you're sure—"

"We'll tell them Finn's my child, that Kieran's the father – and that we know he's taken Finn. That way we can give them more to go on."

Mum gave me a hug. She started to cry, which I was glad about, because she hadn't cried yesterday – it had been me sobbing my heart out – and I knew that Mum was partly crying with relief.

"I want to do it for you two," I said, and I felt really strong and full of courage. "But most of all –" and I took a deep breath to stop my voice going all wobbly – "I want to do it for Finn."

"Enter!" rang the voice. "The door stands wide."

He took a deep breath and stepped in.

The room was small, neat, uncluttered, filled with an extraordinary feeling of peace. Light from two windows spilled on to its wooden floor. White walls stretched to up to thick wooden beams. On one wall hung a simple crucifix. The air smelled of roses and the tang of lavender.

"Daniel?" Sylvia moved swiftly towards him, took his hand in a firm clasp. She was tall, with a heavy body and piercing black eyes. "I am so delighted to meet you."

"Thank you for seeing me."

He felt suddenly small and a bit pathetic. Even as he stood here, in this remote village in the middle of nowhere, armed only with a couple of photos and a grubby teddy bear, gearing himself up to talk in intimate detail about the past few weeks of his life to a total stranger, Finn might be crying for help.

Except as he sat on a chair by the window, opposite Sylvia, she didn't feel like a stranger at all. Her eyes seemed to search his face for something she'd already begun to find.

She said, "There is someone in your own life who has recently passed over to the other side."

His body clenched with fear. "You don't mean Finn is—"

"No, this is not a child . . . She is an elderly lady . . . I can see her spirit as clearly as I see you . . . She is stooped, with a slender body and wonderful green eyes, the same colour as yours . . . Her name . . . I can see an 'A' . . . What more can you tell me?"

And then he understood. He said unsteadily, "The 'A' stands for Alice . . . She's my grandmother . . . She died on the first of May."

"Ah." Sylvia smiled with relief. "You and your Alice, you were very close."

"She was my only family." His voice choked. He hadn't expected any of this.

"Exactly so . . . Alice asks me to send you her love. And her blessing. She wants you to be happy without her."

Sharp tears stung his eyes. "Sometimes that's very hard."

"Of course, I understand. But it will get easier . . . You have Laura . . . She tells me you are very important to her."

"I am?" He felt overwhelmed by the compliment.

"Alice . . . I can hear Alice again. She says she knows you and Laura are great friends. Alice wants you to love her. It would make her very happy if you did."

Tears streamed down his cheeks. "I'll try. I mean . . . I suppose I already do."

"Good. Very good . . . Here, wipe your eyes." She gave him a linen handkerchief, scented with lavender. He buried his face in it.

A gentle pause hung in the air, soothing, refreshing. Daniel crushed the linen in his hand. The room looked brighter, as if the tears had washed dust from his eyes.

"Now." Sylvia pulled a small table towards her. "To the urgent business of the day . . . Tell me about the child who is lost. Tell me of Finn. From the very beginning."

So he did.

"I see. A most interesting story. Thank you."

She drummed her fingers against the arms of her chair, nodding towards Daniel's bag.

"What do you have for me in there?"

"A photo of me and Jade at my school dance . . . A photo of Finn, taken when he was living in Brittany . . . and Finn's favourite bear. Her name's Harriet."

Sylvia propped Harriet on her lap, touching the space which should have been an eye. She looked carefully at each photograph.

"Do you know what Finn was wearing yesterday?"

Trying to keep his voice steady, Daniel recited the details Eve had given him.

Sylvia closed her eyes. For a moment he thought she'd fallen asleep, but although her body was absolutely still, it was also tense and watchful, as though she were listening to the voice of the wind in the trees.

Suddenly a ripple seemed to run through her. Her eyes fluttered open with alarm.

"What can you see?"

"I am not sure. For a brief moment I saw the face of the child, but then a shadow flickered across it. Like the wings of a dark bird. The shadow brings illness. Not death, it is not as stark as that. But there is something unwell surrounding the child."

Her eyes met Daniel's. He was struck once again by their depth and blackness.

"It is most unusual. I have never encountered it before."

"What do you think it can mean?"

She shook her head. "I could not even hazard a guess. But when you find Finn, you will know. All will be made clear. A shadow – an omen – as dark as that cannot remain hidden for long."

Worry clawed at Daniel's stomach.

Sylvia had closed her eyes again.

The peace of the room intensified into silence. Outside a dog barked, a raven cried from the trees. He noticed details in the room: a Bible on a shelf, a vase of white roses. The school-dance photograph stared up at him. He remembered the thunder of music, the heat of their bodies; wondered whether he'd ever hold Jade again.

Sylvia said, "Ah, wait . . . I can see something else . . . Movement, ripples . . . Sunlight, it is glinting on water . . . The child is close to water."

Terror flashed through him. "Do you mean he's going to drown?"

"No. I do not feel he is in danger . . . Quite the opposite. I can hear him laughing, and the sound of someone singing."

Daniel said, "But Jade sings. She has a wonderful voice. Is Finn back with her?"

Sylvia opened her eyes. "No. The voice was a man's, singing an Irish melody."

"And this water . . . Is Finn by the sea? On the coast? Is he in a plane, flying over an ocean?"

Sylvia frowned. "Once again, I do not know. I cannot see any further." The tension in her body seemed to ebb away. "Please, Daniel, accept my apologies. I am suddenly very tired. This takes enormous energy. As I get older, the energy lasts only for short spaces of time." She stood up, held out her hand. "I hope I have helped you."

"Thank you." His lips felt stiff and dry with disappointment. "I hope so too."

"Remember—"

"What?" He looked her squarely, courageously, in the eyes.

"Out of bad always comes good." Her warm smile held the merest hint of pity.

"Yes." He knew he'd heard those very same words from someone else, and quite recently, but he could not remember who or precisely when. His mind seemed to have gone fuzzy and blank. He felt tired and heavy, hungry and desperately thirsty, as if he hadn't eaten or drunk for a week.

He put the photos and Harriet in his bag, picked it up, nodded to Sylvia and turned slowly away.

He closed the door, leaning against it, taking deep breaths, trying to compose himself.

Sickness and water. Omens. A bird with dark wings which cast a flickering shadow. What was he supposed to think? How on earth could he possibly make sense of it?

Sylvia meant well, he was sure of that. But these snippets

of suspicions had made everything feel more precarious than ever, as if he'd been given half a jigsaw puzzle whose pieces would never fit. And he had no *time* to sit and ponder anything!

He walked slowly through the fir-trees. Clusters of ravens gathered overhead, black against the sky, cawing fierce argument and revenge.

Water. Why was Finn near water? Was he in a swimming-pool? On a river somewhere? Playing in a wood, near a stream?

He looked towards the bottom of the path. Laura stood waiting for him. She smiled and waved. He suddenly remembered how she'd blocked his path that evening in Oxford when he'd been trying to follow Kieran.

Where had he been exactly?

Something nudged the corners of his mind. Something important.

Where had he been?

On the edge of Hythe Bridge Street.

Wait a minute . . . What lay *under* the bridge?

The Oxford canal.

And its narrowboats.

On which people lived.

He started to race towards Laura.

She said, "What is it? What's happened? What did Sylvia say?"

"Quick, Laura . . . Just drive . . . I'll tell you in the car."

I dressed in a navy shirt and pleated skirt, dead ordinary, a bit like a school uniform – though for the first time in my life I didn't feel like a school kid.

The police arrived again. Dad was with us this time and it made things easier. I told them the whole story: that I was Finn's mum, Kieran was his dad, we knew that Kieran had taken Finn. We told them that Kieran had been trying to get in touch with me – yes, I suppose it was harassment – that he'd threatened Daniel in town, that we had to assume he'd been stalking me, that he must have seen me and Mum drive off yesterday morning.

Is that all it was: yesterday? It seems so long ago. When you're watching and waiting for someone, every minute feels like a day and a half.

The police were pleased and relieved. They'd no news of Finn, but they said it certainly helped that we'd been straight with them.

We drove to the police station in St Aldates. They said were we ready for the barrage of cameras? I said yes, let's do it as fast as we can. If it only jogged one person's memory and we got a result, it'd be worth it.

I was terribly nervous. My hands felt frozen and I kept wanting to go to the loo.

The police led us into this room and I sat down, Mum and Dad either side of me. All I could think was, *I must not cry, I must get the words out without breaking down.*

"Tell them the facts," the policewoman said. "Make the story as clear and simple as you can. Tell them Finn was snatched from his nursery. We know that the man who took him was his father and looked very like Finn. We'll flash up the photograph. We'll give people a number to ring if they think they have any information. And we'll get you on the local news at midday, and again throughout the evening news bulletins on local TV if we haven't had a result by then.

"Good luck, Jade. We'll be monitoring the calls."

I managed to get through it without bursting into tears.

The hardest part was saying Finn's name, telling everyone what he'd been wearing. Once I'd actually said, "He's my little boy, and I want him back with me more than anything in the world," I knew I'd never have to pretend about him again.

The feeling of relief — well, it's hard to describe. I hadn't realised what a strain it had been, living the lie, hoping nobody in London would guess I was pregnant, hoping that nobody would suspect Kieran was the father. And those years in France, never being able to admit to anyone that I was Finn's mum, having to watch what I said every minute of the day.

Afterwards, the policewoman said I'd done a great job. We were to go home and try to get some rest.

I went straight up to Finn's room on my own for a bit, until I managed to stop crying. Then I ripped off that skirt and blouse and threw them in the washing basket. They smelled of the police station. I pulled on some jeans and an old T-shirt and stared at myself in the mirror.

Everybody knows . . .

When we find Finn, when he's safely home with me again, I'm going to tell him I'm his mum.

I want him to know.

Just the minute he gets home.

So *that's* what the boy had been doing that afternoon.

Following Kieran.

If only he'd *told* me, we could have chased after him together.

Of course, I blame myself again – this time for getting in his way. If I hadn't arrived on the scene, maybe Daniel would have found out where Kieran lives and we wouldn't still be trying to find him!

Although there's no guarantee he'll be anywhere near the canal. I've got a nasty feeling about Kieran. He's the kind who can be totally unpredictable. Here one minute, gone the next. Walked away from his teaching post without any warning. Abandoned Jade without a second glance. Capable of throwing poor little Finn into a clapped-out car and driving him to the back of beyond with never a by-your-leave.

Some men get away with murder . . .

No, delete that. Scrub it out. I didn't even think it. Please God, let me not think the unthinkable.

I drove as fast as I could from Eastleach Turville, back to

Chalfont Road. At least, I *tried* to. I couldn't do anything about the tractor that had broken down near the Burford roundabout. I told the boy to stop fretting, but it was so frustrating, having to wait like that.

We didn't get into Oxford until 12.30. I said, did he want me to drop him on Hythe Bridge Street? He said no, he'd go back to Clare and Martin's and check for messages. Then he'd get on his bike.

I asked him whether he was going to tell Jade about Sylvia.

"What's the point?" he said. "I may be on a wild-goose chase. Jade may not approve of Sylvia. I don't know how she feels about all that stuff. I don't know how *I* feel about it. Jade may be furious with me again, accuse me of betraying her behind her back."

He was clasping and unclasping his hands: as I drove, I could see them out of the corner of my eye.

"If I find Kieran and Finn on the canal—"

"Don't tackle Kieran on your own."

"Why? Do you think he could be dangerous?"

"You never know. Please, Daniel, don't risk it."

I dropped him outside Clare and Martin's.

"Ring me the minute you have news."

"I will. Thanks for your help, Laura. You've been great."

He kissed my cheek, and I blushed.

I pointed to his bag. "Don't forget Harriet."

I watched him stumble into the house.

I wanted to go in with him, but I hadn't been invited.

Daniel

Clare called, "Danny? Is that you?"

He cursed under his breath. The last thing he wanted was having to explain to Clare why he was in such a frantic hurry.

"Yes. Have there been any messages?"

Clare pounded upstairs from the kitchen.

"No calls, nothing . . . Danny, what's going on? Why didn't you *tell* us?"

His heart missed several beats. "Tell you what?"

"I've just seen the midday news on TV . . . Jade's broadcast an appeal for Finn."

"She has?" His hands pricked with pins and needles.

"She said that Finn's her son . . . Did you know?"

"Yes, I did," he said wildly. "But they kept it secret . . . I couldn't tell you . . . Jade didn't want anyone to know."

"I'm not surprised." The corner of Clare's mouth twitched. "It must have been hard for her to go public like she has . . . Of course I'm not *blaming* you for keeping a confidence. Those poor people must be going though hell."

"Yes."

The pins and needles seemed to spread up his arms and down his spine.

"You're white as a sheet. Come on, I'll make you a cup of tea and a sandwich."

"But I haven't the time . . . I've been talking to somone . . . I may have a lead on where Finn's been taken. I've got to cycle into Oxford."

She grasped his arm. "The way you look at the moment, you'll fall off your bike before you've reached the top of the road. How will *that* help Finn, I'd like to know?"

His legs shook. "Well . . ."

Clare seized the advantage. "Come on, Danny. Downstairs. You're not going anywhere until you've had something to eat . . . And you've told me *exactly* what's been happening to those Davenports."

After lunch, which he devoured in ten minutes while talking non-stop and drinking the most refreshing mug of tea in the world, Clare hugged him, told him to tread very carefully if he was going to continue to play private detective on his own.

He smiled bleakly at her. He hadn't told her about Sylvia — or where he was going now.

That would have been tempting fate.

Nor had he told Laura about Sylvia's premonition of Finn not being well. After all, it had only been a hunch. Laura was frantic with worry about all this. What was the point in giving her something else to fret about?

He tucked the photo of Finn into his pocket, climbed stiffly on his bike and cycled past Jade's. He didn't want to tell her where he was going either.

Not yet.

If his mission drew a blank, he'd rather she didn't know about it than falsely raise her hopes. She must be shattered after the appeal – and if there'd been any news of Finn, she'd have told him.

He'd cycle to Hythe Bridge Street, leave his bike by the canal. Then he'd walk along the towpath as slowly as he could, keeping his eyes peeled. Please God he'd find *something*, some clue – anything – that would lead him to Finn.

He padlocked his bike to the railings above the canal, his fingers shaking with haste.

He shoved his hands into his pockets and began to saunter as nonchalantly as he could down the towpath. Its puddles glistened with last night's rain.

The river flowed gently on his left. To his right, the canal lay flat, its water a dark yellowy green, thick with sludge and weed.

He walked past the first of the narrowboats. Its name, *My Watery Haven*, had been lovingly painted on its navy wood in swirly gold letters. Its roof groaned with sacks of winter coal, pots of flowering plants, an old lifebelt and a rusty watering-can. Blue and white check curtains, firmly drawn, masked the windows.

On the next, *Ice Maiden*, a young man in a faded brown beret sat reading. But as Daniel passed him, he felt a faint hostility, as if the man's eyes were not on his book but drilling into Daniel's back, warning him off.

On *Mrs Tiggywinkle*, the mouth-watering scent of frying bacon drifted from the kitchen. A white cat yawned and stretched in the sun; washing flapped on a line. A girl sat knitting while her dad tinkered with the insides of a radio.

Daniel looked along the canal. The narrowboats were moored end to end, as far as his eye could see.

There must be fourteen or fifteen of them, stretching all the way to the next bridge. What am I going to do? Start asking people on them whether they've seen Finn?

What if Kieran has friends here who know what he's done? My asking questions might alert them, give them the chance to warn him.

*

He reached Isis Lock, leaned against the bridge and took stock.

Mallards and coots clucked along the banks; office workers wandered down the towpath, eating sandwiches; joggers puffed by, pouring sweat. The narrowboats gently heaved against the thick ropes of their moorings, their windows twinkling in the sun. Plumes of smoke trailed from their chimneys as stoves dried out the effects of last night's storm.

Daniel could not decide what to do. If he was going to search for Finn, he'd have to go from boat to boat, tapping at windows. Or he'd have to climb aboard, without invitation, cram his head through the door, wave the photograph and say, "Excuse me, but have you seen this child?"

It seemed an outrageous way to behave. This tiny waterworld looked so sane, so enchanting. It couldn't possibly be the stuff of kidnap and blackmail.

Yet the bridge had been where Kieran had vanished.

And Sylvia said she'd seen water.

He had no choice but to try.

He walked purposefully towards the boat that lay in front of him.

A man stood at the open door, jabbering into a mobile

phone. Daniel held up the photo of Finn, pointed to it, mouthed, "Have you seen this child?"

The man shook his head, shrugged his shoulders, turned his back and continued his conversation.

Thanks for nothing!

He walked towards the next boat, tapped at a window, climbed across a plank onto the boat and knocked at the door. There was no answer. Something threatening about the silence made him feel uncomfortable. He scuttled back to the towpath.

The next narrowboat, *The Great Escape*, lay hidden behind dense overgrown brambles and wild geranium. Striped muslin curtains shrouded the windows. The contents of its roof gave little away: a battered hosepipe, a bundle of chopped wood and an ancient mackintosh huddled across it.

He didn't feel like tapping on the door.

This is useless. A complete waste of time. I'll never find them.

He'd almost turned away altogether – the boat was so obviously closed and empty – when he spotted something underneath the mackintosh.

A scarlet sweater. One sleeve lay along the wood like a motionless snake.

Daniel froze.

Kieran had worn a scarlet sweater the day he'd vanished.

Was this just a coincidence? Desperate as he was to find *anything*, was he now merely clutching at straws?

The boat looked so private, so secretive. Could this be where Kieran had taken Finn? Were they inside? If they were, how could he prove it without banging down the door?

Nothing would feel better, right now!

He remembered Laura's warning: "Don't tackle Kieran on your own."

He stepped away from the boat, checking the windows. Through one of the curtains he could see a chink of light – but nothing more. No voices, no chimney smoke, no rattle of cooking pans, no scent of food.

But suddenly there was something else.

The beautiful lilting notes of a flute, clear, plangent, lovingly confident, rang into the air.

Someone had begun to play "Greensleeves" on a flute.

It could only be Kieran McVeigh.

I was frantic to do *something* to ease the pain, so I started to clean Finn's room, to tidy his clothes and toys.

I sorted through everything in his chest of drawers, matched the socks, tucked the pairs into each other. I put together the pieces of his favourite wooden puzzle: an orange elephant standing in a jungle of blue leaves. I washed his paintbrushes until they were soft and fluffy. I stuck his latest painting on the wall above his bed. I shuffled his books and propped them neatly on the shelf.

It was like everything I touched brought him closer.

Then the phone rang. I flew downstairs. I recognised the voice immediately. It was Alison's.

Ally and I were best friends when I lived in Camden Town. She said she'd seen me on TV, got my number from directory enquiries. Said she hoped I wouldn't mind if she rang. She couldn't *believe* I'd had a baby; she was so sorry to hear the terrible news about the kidnap.

And then came the crunch: me and Kieran! What on *earth* had been going on?

It felt so weird talking to her again.

It took me straight back to being thirteen, with my head crammed to bursting with the latest gossip and make-up and fashion, what was cool and what wasn't.

I cut Ally off as quickly as I could. OK, I'd admitted Finn was my child, but that didn't mean I was going to start blabbing about him to anyone who asked. And as for *talking* about Kieran and how I'd felt about him – in your dreams. If I'd managed to keep it to myself at the time, why would I want to open the wounds now?

There was no way Ally and I could ever be friends again. It was like talking to a voice from another planet.

I put the phone down and suddenly I was *dying* to see Daniel. I'd been in such a state yesterday, taken everything out on him. Given him such a hard time.

I knew he was totally on my side, that he'd do anything to help.

I told Mum I was going over the road to see him.

But when I did, Clare said he'd gone off on his bike.

She'd seen the appeal too. Said she was desperately sorry and if there was *anything* she could do . . .

Soon everyone will know.

I couldn't face going home. I knew there might be more phone calls from well-wishers, but I didn't want to talk to anyone.

All I wanted was my Finn – and my Daniel.

I thought, *What if Kieran decides to take Finn back to the nursery? What if he's sorry for snatching him like that?*

I don't know, I suppose it was a crazy thing to hope for. But I darted into the garage, grabbed my bike and started cycling towards the Banbury Road.

At least it was something to *do* . . .

He raced back along the towpath, splashing though the puddles; ripped the padlock from his bike; cycled like a crazy thing to Jade's.

Eve answered the door. She looked exhausted, her forehead creased with anxious lines, her lips pale and dry. Bobby Davenport hovered behind her, then crashed away into the kitchen.

"Daniel! Where's Jade?"

"I've come to ask you the same thing. I haven't seen her since yesterday."

"She went over to yours an hour ago."

"I've been out looking for Finn."

"Any joy?"

"I'm not sure . . . I may have found something."

"Should we tell the police?"

"No, not yet. I must tell Jade first."

She looked at him uncertainly. "Come in and wait . . . I'm sure she won't be long."

He hesitated, but only for a moment. "Thanks, Eve, but I think I'll go round the block, try to track her down . . ."

*

For an hour, he cycled the streets.

Finally, he made for Chalfont Road again. Just as he reached the top, he spotted Jade wearily pedalling towards home.

He zoomed towards her. "Where have you been?"

She screeched her bike to a halt. "I went to the nursery to talk to the teachers, try to pick up some clues. It didn't help. I couldn't bear looking at the other kids when my Finn wasn't with them . . . After that I just cycled the streets, looking for him in a hopeless kind of way."

She bit her lip. He could see dust in her hair, a streak of dirt trickling down her neck. He straddled his bike and grasped her arm.

"Listen . . . I may know where Finn is."

"*What?*" Colour flooded her face.

"Don't get too excited. I haven't actually *seen* him . . . But I think I heard Kieran playing his flute!"

"Where?"

"Start cycling . . . I'll tell you on the way. We've got to get down to the canal, the bit near the Isis Lock. It'll be quickest to go into town . . ."

As they reached the canal, Daniel said, "Let's pedal along the towpath. We may need to grab Finn and make a really fast getaway . . . I can sit him in my bike basket."

They set off along the path, Daniel leading, weaving carefully out of the way of walkers, joggers, other cyclists. The boats seemed deserted, though he didn't have time to look at them with any care. He craned his neck towards *The Great Escape*.

But when they reached Isis Lock, Daniel screeched his brakes. The brambles and wild geranium lining that section of the bank drooped over empty water.

The narrowboat had vanished.

Aghast, Daniel said, "I don't believe it! The boat was here . . . I didn't imagine it . . . Look, you can see the space it's left."

Jade ran a sleeve over her perspiring cheeks. "So where's the bastard gone?"

"Maybe he saw me on the towpath. Maybe I frightened him away."

"But you said he started playing the flute." She was close to tears. "Why would he have done that if he'd *seen* you?"

"You're right. He'd hardly have been tempting me on board!"

"So where is he now?" She brushed her fingers over her eyes and swore. "*Where is my Finn?*"

Daniel reached out and touched her shoulder. "Kieran

can't have gone far – or fast. The boats chug really slowly, at less than walking pace. Let's cycle along the towpath until we catch them up."

"And then what? Throw ourselves into the canal? Swim after him?"

"Let's find the boat first," Daniel said firmly. "Then we can decide what to do."

They mounted their bikes again and began to cycle along the towpath.

As Oxford dwindled behind them, the landscape changed. On their right they zoomed past Castlemill Boatyard; elegant new flats; the walls of an ancient factory; town-house gardens sprawling down to the canal; a sports centre and a cricket pitch.

On their left, fields and the railway line beckoned to the sky. A train roared by, flinging its reverberating echo in its wake.

Other narrowboats lay moored along the canal, but they looked rougher, less comfortable dwellings. Some lay rotting and abandoned altogether. Near Wolvercote, a boat chugged towards them, a swarthy woman guiding its tiller.

She must've seen The Great Escape *coming towards her . . . Should I yell out and ask her? Maybe not.*

Jade called from behind him, "How much further? My legs are killing me."

He scanned the empty water. "Keep going . . . We must be getting close."

He pedalled on, bumping over the stony path, aware that he was tired too. He could hear Jade's panting breath and then her shout of, "Daniel! Stop!"

His brakes squealed. "What's the matter?" He looked at her over his shoulder.

"I must have a puncture . . . I can't go any further."

He slipped off his bike and examined the tyre. Shreds of rubber poked away from it like the legs of a dead spider.

"Leave the bike behind that hedge . . . We'll have to go the rest of the way on foot . . . Come on, Jade . . . Hurry . . . We must be close to him by now."

They raced along the path, Daniel wheeling his bike, its pedals bumping painfully against his legs. His sprained ankle ached and a stitch in his side began to bite.

He raised his head. "There!" He pointed towards the bridge. "Look, Jade, over there!"

The Great Escape lay inside Wolvercote Lock.

Kieran stood on the bank.

"Quick, he hasn't seen us . . . One last spurt. We'll be able to get on to the boat before he takes it any further."

He flung his bike across the path.

"Quick, before he sees us."

He grabbed her hand.

"Jump, Jade, jump!"

They flung themselves onto *The Great Escape*.

Kieran, stooping over the lock, lifted his head, pushed his hair out of his eyes and spotted them.

"Well, *well*," he sang out. "How *exceptionally* clever of you to find me. May I welcome you aboard?"

Jade screamed, "*You bastard!* Where's Finn? What have you done with him?"

Kieran straightened his back, swaggered triumphantly towards her.

He stepped lightly and gracefully onto the boat, steadied himself and smiled.

"Hello, Jade. It's good to see you too."

Part of me wanted to hurl myself at Kieran, beat him to a pulp, push him overboard and watch him drown.

I've never felt such fury in my life.

I screamed at him, "What have you done with my child?"

He said in that beautiful soft Irish voice, "Oh, come on, Jade. He's my child too. Tell me he's my child."

His hair tumbled to his shoulders, his eyes glinted at me, pale and sparkling. He was flirting with me! My legs were trembling and I thought my heart would pound its way out of my body. The anger was all mixed up with the thrill of seeing him again – and the pull of that chemistry between us.

I know he felt it too.

He moved towards me – we were so close on that tiny boat – and I almost fell into his arms.

I was lucky to have Daniel beside me, his hand on my shoulder. He said with an icy calm, "Just tell us where Finn is. The police know all about you. Jade's broadcast an appeal. There's no great escape now, Kieran. *What have you done with Finn?*"

Kieran heard what Daniel said, but it was like *I'd* asked the question. Kieran's eyes never left my face.

"Finnegan's in my bed. He's taking a wee nap. I haven't harmed a hair of his head. We've had a glorious time together."

I turned to crash through the door of the boat. I couldn't wait another second to see my Finn again, make sure that he was safe. Even then I wasn't sure that Kieran was telling me the truth. But he moved faster than I did, fast as a snake in the grass. He stood in front of the door and blocked my way.

His eyes glittered at me, a warning behind them.

"Before you take him away in your loving arms, I'd much appreciate a quick word. There are things I need to tell you." He shot Daniel a filthy look. "Just the two of us. In private."

I spluttered, "Daniel's not going anywhere without me. And I'm not leaving without Finn. So whatever you've got to say to me, say it now to both of us. And make it quick."

Kieran shrugged. "Have it your way. But this may take a little while. If you insist on keeping this young man of yours around, won't you both step inside? I have to steer the boat through the lock, moor her to the bank."

I shouted, "Then hurry *up*."

He remained completely unruffled. "Go in and take a seat.

Pour yourselves some coffee. Make yourselves at home." He was mocking us now. "Please, be my guests."

I was shaking with fury and exhaustion – and relief.

Kieran moved away from the door to let me pass.

Daniel muttered, "Don't let him get to you. He knows he's beaten . . . Quick, let's get inside before he changes his mind."

We pushed our way through the narrow door, down three little steps, into an untidy miniature world.

Beneath its low ceiling, dusty wooden chairs and an old sofa lined the walls. Sunlight twinkled through the windows onto piles of possessions – shoes, books, cushions, papers, tins, boxes – crammed into every corner.

I could hear the persistent buzz of the engine thrumming against the water beneath us like a giant bumblebee, echoing the throbbing anger in my heart.

I crashed my way down the narrow corridor at the centre of the boat: past the chairs and the stove, past a small desk with a computer, through the galley kitchen, past a basin, a tiny loo and a bath, into – at last – an open area with a bed.

Finn lay fast asleep under a soft cream blanket.

He looked so enchanting it made my heart stop altogether: his thumb half in his mouth, his cheeks flushed, his dark hair curling on the pillow, his breath coming sweet and evenly.

I started to cry with joy. In my worst nightmare, I'd imagined I might never see him again.

I longed to pick him up and crush him in my arms.

But I thought, *I must find out what Kieran wants with me. I have to finish this, once and for all.*

So I said, ever so softly, "Sleep tight, my darling. Mummy's here for you."

Then I turned and tiptoed away.

It was one of the hardest things I've ever had to do.

I climbed back to the sluice gate, the windlass clenched in my hand.

I cranked away at the lock — it's the stiffest on the canal — cursing under my breath. All I could think was, *That young man of Jade's gets on my wick. Why hasn't he got the decency to leave us alone? What in the name of God is any of this to do with him?*

I leaped back onto *The Great Escape*, steered it towards the bank, slung its rope good and tight around a mooring ring, and went back to turn off the engine. Oh, it was lovely and peaceful when the chugging stopped.

It was only a spur of the moment decision to snatch Finn.

Sure, I'd followed Jade several times since I'd seen her in Cornmarket. Carefully, mind, very carefully. Most of the time she didn't have a clue. I wanted to catch her unawares, but yesterday, when I watched her drive away with her mother, I thought something might be up — that I might have a chance to meet the wee child on his own.

Just him and me.

I reckoned we'd have about twenty-four hours on the boat before anyone twigged where we were. Then I'd have to scarper. I thought with a bit of luck we could get all the way to Thrupp, in the depths of Oxfordshire. It's one of my favourite canal journeys — and it's marvellously quiet out there. Nobody would spot us when we were on the move. It would probably take us three hours. Finn would enjoy the ride once he'd had his nap.

Me and the wee boy, we played on deck this morning, happy as sandboys. Well, I couldn't keep him shut inside all day, now could I? It wouldn't have been fair, with him brimming with energy and curiosity. So I took him out in the sunshine, in my arms, pointing out the water and the ducks and the other boats.

It's a brilliant little world of its own, the canal community. I've been coming here, every summer, for ten years, since I was seventeen. I suppose Jade and her young man must be the same age as I was when I first came here . . .

One of my best friends, Robin, he owns this boat. He goes hitchhiking around Europe in August and lets me look after it. I love being on water, the smell of the weed, the warm summer rain on the canal, the clucking of moorhens. It soothes away your worries like nothing else I know.

I didn't let go of Finnegan. Not for a moment. I couldn't be having him tipping over the edge.

Proud as punch I was of him. Passers-by stared at us, smiled and waved.

I expect one of them grassed me up.

Sure, every so often Finnegan would ask, "Where's my mummy? And where's Jay? When are they coming for me?"

But I just told him, "Soon. They'll be here soon, little Finnegan."

He seemed happy enough with that.

I have to hand it to Jade. She's done a grand job with the wee boy. Even if he does seem to think that Jade's his big sister . . . It's not exactly *my* place to tell him the truth, is it? I suppose they think, what does it matter, they're all just one big happy family.

And where does that leave me?

Completely out of the picture, that's for sure.

Did I have plans for us? For me and the child?

Hardly. I knew we'd only have a couple of days together, at the very most. I didn't want to think any further.

How *could* I have proper plans? Until a couple of weeks ago, I'd never in the world dreamed that Finn existed. I just wanted to have him to myself for a few precious hours.

Enough to shake Jade up, warn her in no uncertain terms that I *had* to see her. Like I told her young man in Oxford, it was a matter of necessity.

More than that.

It's life and death . . .

I reckon I'll have to start from the beginning, so I'll make better sense, so you'll understand entirely what this unholy mess is all about.

It's not of my wanting or my making. You can call it Fate if you like. The luck – or the ill luck – of the draw.

In your pool of genes. The lucky dip.

Not that I knew anything about it until I'd got back to my flat from Jade's in Camden Town. The night we'd had sex. How in the name of God was I to know that three hours later my mother would ring me, and my life would never be the same again?

I was so full of remorse when I left Jade's I thought I'd burst open and flood down the drain. Maybe I even *wanted* to disappear without trace. I'd never done anything like that before – or since. I sat in the car outside my flat and cried. It used to take a lot to make me cry like that . . .

Not any more.

I mean, it wasn't totally my fault, but I guess I could have stopped it. I'm well aware of that. I knew Jade was only thirteen, that I was ten years older — that the ultimate responsibility was mine. I could have let her get out of the car. I could have driven away. But I saw her to the door, like a gentleman.

And she reached up and kissed me on the mouth.

That was the moment I realised: I wasn't going to be able to resist.

I knew she had a crush on me. But Mother of God, so did lots of the girls. As a teacher, you're in a powerful position. It can easily go to your head. They think you're a role model, a hero — and soon, if you're not careful, *you* think so too.

I'd just graduated from music college and it was my first teaching job. So all that adulation, I wasn't used to it. You have to play it down. You learn to ignore it. You try to treat them all the same, tell yourself not to have favourites. You smile at them all. You make sure you're never alone with them — that the opportunity to take things further simply doesn't exist.

But Jade's singing voice, it was something else. That very first day, in our first lesson together, she opened her mouth and this sound came out of it, pure as the driven snow.

I thought, *Sweet Jesus! What have we got here?*

I wanted to listen to her all the day and through the long dark night. I wanted to see those golden eyes of hers follow my every movement as she sang. She was beautiful — her adorable little face, her body, the way her hair swung like a waterfall down to her waist. It wasn't just her voice.

And I wanted to write songs for her, first the music, then the lyrics. She doesn't know this — I've never dared tell her — but that first day we met, I drove home and in my head I already had a song I was writing, specially and only for her.

You don't believe me, do you? You've written me off as some foul, lecherous guy, one of those filthy paedophiles you read about in the newspaper, those maniacs who deal in pornography on the Internet, flashing up naked bodies of defenceless children, trading their innocence.

I'll prove to you I'm nothing like that. Here's the song I wrote for Jade the first day I met her. It took me weeks to polish it. But this is what she sang at the Christmas concert to my flute. It was the highlight of the evening, everyone said so. If you could've heard the applause . . . understood something of how I was feeling just then.

Nightingale

Sing for me, sing for me, over the hill,
Sing when the corn is ripe, golden and still,
Sing for the apple tree's blossom and then
Sing for me over and over again.

Now is the time for you, most blessed bird,
Sing for we need you, I give you the word,
I make intercession, I listen, and then
Ask: sing for us over and over again.

Sing when the nights are long, high on the moon,
Sing when our troubles come only too soon.
Sing for our purity, celebrate calm,
Stand for integrity, pour on its balm.

Sing in our dawning and through into dusk,
Watch as the perfumes of night drench their musk,
Sing for remembrance, be proud of our past
But as we look forward, we also stand fast.

Sing for us, sing for us, over the hill,
Sing when the corn is ripe, golden and still,
Sing for the apple tree's blossom and then
Come: sing for me over and over again.

I can tell you from my heart it was one of the greatest nights of my life.

The concert was the culmination of my first term's work. The school had never heard anything like it before. I'd raised their standards to something they'd only dreamed of.

How did I follow that?

I slept with Jade.

It was like I'd fallen from a state of grace. Because hard on the heels of Jade and me having sex came that call from my mother.

"I've been ringing and ringing," she said.

I hardly recognised her voice, it was so thick with weeping.

"It's your dad. He's poorly."

I switched on the lamp. "What's happened?"

"I knew something was wrong, but neither of us wanted to face it. He's been so moody, not sleeping at night, taking cat-naps all through the day instead – not himself at all. He's lost a lot of weight. He keeps forgetting things: where he's put something, what he's said to me." There was a pause. "I told the doctors everything I could . . . But I never suspected this."

"What's *wrong*, Mother?"

"We found out today . . . Your father has Huntington's."

"What?"

"It's a condition that affects the brain." Now she was sobbing. "The nerve cells in the brain die, and nothing can replace them . . . Nobody's discovered a cure."

"Mother of God . . ."

"Please, Kieran . . . Can you come home?"

"What, *now*?"

I was still confused, alarmed, filling up with this terrible black dread.

"Now, this very minute. It's an emergency. I can't possibly cope without you. You'll have to come home."

I thought, *Mother of God, forgive me. This is my punishment.*

Kieran moored the boat and switched off the engine.

We sat in a circle on *The Great Escape* in the kind of dreadful silence that eats away at you.

Daniel and I sat on the little sofa, Kieran in a chair next to the stove. He'd poured us large bowls of coffee, strong and sweet and black, the best I've ever tasted.

Moorhens clucked on the canal, water rippled outside the windows, the clock ticked on the wall. I could see Kieran's flute in its case, hanging from a peg.

If I were to tell you that it felt like home, you'd only laugh at me.

But it did.

Except that Kieran was glaring at Daniel, and Daniel scowled back. The boat was so narrow their legs were almost touching. Kieran scraped his hair back with his fingers, secured it in a ponytail with an elastic band.

I sat there feeling shattered. I was long past fury, anger, recrimination. I was totally exhausted. The journey to London, the shock of Finn's disappearance, the sleepless night, the TV appeal, cycling around Chalfont Road and north Oxford and then down to the canal — it all flashed through my head and my body, draining it of strength.

I felt as if I'd never stand up again.

But I knew I had to get this stuff with Kieran over and done with. So I took a huge gulp of coffee and I asked him straight.

"Why have you made us come here? Why have you done this? I haven't spent a night away from Finn since he was born."

Kieran said, "I'm truly sorry, Jade," and his face was very pale.

"Have you *any* idea what the last twenty-four hours have been like? What kind of things I imagined might have happened?"

"Little Finnegan was never in any danger —"

"But I didn't *know* that, did I? Why have you *done* this?"

He looked across at me. There was something in his eyes I'd never seen before: a kind of helplessness. His lips were trembling and his hands were clenched into tight fists.

"Because I'm dying," he said.

The boat swayed around me, but I wouldn't let myself give in.

I said bitterly, "I wish! . . . Don't be ridiculous."

Daniel put a hand on my arm, as if to say, *Wait a minute, listen.*

228

"Oh, I don't mean *immediately*," Kieran said, his voice grim. "Nobody knows how long it might take. That's one of the dreadful things about this disease. But I've had all the tests. Months of them. There's nothing more I can do. It's been confirmed."

"Why are you talking in riddles? *What's* been confirmed?"

"I've got Huntington's disease. I've inherited the gene from my father. It's the reason I left my teaching post and never came back . . . never got in touch with you again. My mother was at breaking point. I had to go home to look after my parents. I've lived with them ever since. Except for a few weeks every summer, when I come down here, meet up with some of my old schoolfriends, go busking on the streets."

It was like the implications of what Kieran was saying refused to sink in. Daniel's hand tightened on my arm as if to warn me, but I floundered on.

I said, "Look, I'm not interested in talking about the past. Guys who treat people in the way you treated me don't deserve to be heard. I'm sorry your father's ill. And I'm sorry you're sick. But none of this has anything to do with me. Or with Finn. None of this explains your kidnapping Finn. None of it excuses your blackmailing me. If you think you're going to make me feel sorry for you so that everything's forgiven, you're making a big mistake."

Kieran leaned towards me. "OK, I know I behaved like a bastard. We should never have slept together —" his eyes glittered at me with their old seductive fire — "although if I remember rightly at the time you didn't exactly object."

I wanted to slap his face, but Daniel held me back.

"But the reason I had to see you, talk to you, is that I felt you *had* to know."

"Know *what*?"

And suddenly I felt sick.

Kieran stood up. He turned his back on us and stared out of the window.

"You see, Jade."

The lovely Irish lilt in his voice gilded his brutal words like treacle.

"If *I've* got Huntington's, our little Finnegan might have inherited it from me. There's a fifty-fifty chance that he might have it too."

Daniel

He'd been hoping against hope that Sylvia had been only partly right about the shadow of sickness.

She'd seen water.

She'd guided him to the canal.

But when Jade said that Finn was sleeping peacefully in Kieran's bed, Daniel had breathed a sigh of relief. He'd thought Finn might have a rash and a high temperature, whooping cough, measles – the whole range of childhood diseases had flashed through his mind while he'd cycled to and from Oxford.

He'd never imagined anything like this.

Jade said wildly, "Fifty-fifty?"

"I'm afraid so."

"So how will I know whether he—"

Kieran said, "You won't. At least, not yet. You can't do anything until he's eighteen. Then, if you want to tell him about me, about the disease, he can make up his own mind. Whether or not to have the tests." He swung round to face her. "A lot of people prefer not to, choose to ignore the whole thing . . . But who knows, there may even be a cure by then . . . The wonders of modern medicine and all that."

Jade sat with her head in her hands. She seemed bereft of words.

To fill the awful silence, Daniel looked at Kieran. "How *is* your father?"

Kieran gave him a fleeting smile. "It's good of you to ask." His voice choked. "The nurses all say 'as well as can be expected' . . . It's terrible to watch. His speech is so slurred we can hardly understand him. The way he moves – he can't coordinate his arms and legs, the expressions on his face. At times he flings himself about the room like a wild animal. It's as if we're living with a man we barely recognise . . . We do everything we can for him, but every week he gets a little worse."

Daniel said, "How long—"

"Could it go on?" Kieran finished his sentence, his voice dark and bitter. "You tell me. Nobody knows. He could live for years . . . He could die tomorrow."

Jade lifted her head. "I can't stand any more of this . . . I'm taking Finn home."

"Yes." Kieran held out his arms. "I wish I didn't have to tell you all this. I wish things could have been different between us."

Jade refused to look at him.

She turned to Daniel. She hissed, "Get him out of my sight."

Kieran gasped, "Oh, come *on*, Jade . . ."

But she'd raced into the bedroom.

A minute later she was back, Finn in her arms, his sleeping face lying on her shoulder.

Kieran said quietly, "Please don't go like this . . . Can I see you again? Can I see the wee child, just one more time?"

"It's too late, Kieran." Jade pushed past him. "I won't press charges with the police. I'm going to try to forget this ever happened . . . You can count yourself lucky . . . Harassment, abduction –" her eyes flared at him – "sexual assault, you name it – we could chuck it at you."

"*Please*, Jade, don't—"

"I won't. But only on one condition."

"Which is?"

"That you leave us alone." Kieran quailed under her glance. "The police know all about you –" her voice was low and bitter – "so you'd better go and talk to them before they track you down . . . Or before somebody sees you and tells the press they've found the baby-snatcher!"

"But I'm *not*—"

"You'd better do whatever you can to clear your name.

And your story had better be good. You've got one hell of a lot to answer for."

Kieran was shaking. "Please don't *despise* me . . ."

Jade's fingers were threaded through Finn's curls, as if she were protecting him from the words which flew around his head. She had stopped listening to Kieran. "And this thing about Huntington's. It goes no further. I'm not telling my parents. Nobody else but Daniel will know until Finn's old enough to be told. But I'm warning you, Kieran. *Leave us alone.*"

And she was gone.

Kieran was crying now, his eyes blurry, his cheeks wet.

He grasped Daniel's arm.

"Tell Jade I meant her no harm." He crushed his hands together, as if in prayer. "She listens to you. Just give her my love. Tell her I meant her no harm. I'm sorry about what happened. So sorry. I behaved like a total shit. It wasn't her fault, it was mine. But I love that wee child. Will you tell her that? Will you promise me?"

Daniel turned away.

He swallowed back his anger, clenching his fists, forcing himself to give Kieran one last, compassionate answer.

"OK," he said.

But his voice came thin and harsh, and didn't sound like his.

I stood on the towpath, Finn heavy and sleeping in my arms.

I called for Daniel.

More than anything, I wanted him beside me.

If it hadn't been for him, I'd still be pedalling the streets of Oxford, searching for Finn.

Daniel climbed out of the boat. He was holding Finn's folded-up pushchair. He dropped it on the path and took us both in his arms.

We stood there in a little huddle, oblivious of everyone and everything.

Then Daniel said, "Come on. Put Finn in my bike basket. We can rescue your bike tomorrow. Let's go home."

"The police," I said. "We can tell them the panic's over."

"Yes."

"And I don't want to take anything any further . . . No charges of any kind." I hugged Finn more closely. "Do you think I'm right? Do you think Kieran will leave us alone?"

Daniel said slowly, "I think he's really sorry, Jade. Just now, he said he wants you to know he's sorry, that he behaved like a shit, that he really loves Finn." He swallowed. "I'm not sticking up for him, nothing like that . . . But maybe we should give him a chance to prove he'll keep his word."

Relief flooded through me. "Yes. At least we know why he wanted to talk to me!" I shuddered. "That terrible disease."

"But Finn may escape it . . . Don't forget, the chances are even."

"Please God, after all this, he may still be lucky . . ."

"Look at everything that's happened to us in the last few weeks."

"Yes." I nodded, wanting to cry but holding it all inside me.

"Who's to say what could happen in the next fifteen years?"

I said, "I must just keep on hoping."

"If you like, I can do some research, find out more about it . . . If you don't want your parents to know, you'll hardly want books on Huntington's littering the house."

"Would you?"

"Of course." He hugged me again. "Your parents will go crazy with joy that we've got Finn back . . . So will Laura. I must ring her . . . It's her we have to thank . . . her and Sylvia."

Finn stirred and stretched, opened his eyes. "'Lo, Jay. 'Lo, Dan. I was on that boat."

"I know, sweetheart. But now you're back with us."

We hugged him more closely still, and stared down at *The Great Escape*.

Into the sky floated the notes of a flute.

I could feel myself blushing.

"That's the song Kieran wrote for me, the one I sang at the school concert that night. He's playing it deliberately. He's playing it for me."

"I don't care what he's playing," Daniel said.

He kissed my mouth.

"There'll only be the moon to hear it . . . I'm taking you home."

That night, when he was safely tucked up in bed, I told Finn I was his mum.

I said I hadn't wanted to tell him before, but now he was such a big boy, and he'd had such a big adventure on his own, on a boat and all, now that he went to nursery and had lots of big friends, I wanted him to know.

I wanted him to call me Mummy. *My* mummy was his Granny Eve and my daddy was his Grandpa Bobby. *His* daddy — well, his daddy didn't live with us because he'd gone on a long journey to somewhere far away.

Finn thought about it all for a long time, sucking his

thumb, holding Harriet, gazing at me with those beautiful blue-green eyes.

I thought, *It'll be fifteen years before I can tell Finn about Huntington's, about Kieran, about how it all happened. And why ...*

That's nearly half my life all over again.

I wonder where I'll be when I tell him.

And I wonder whether Daniel and I will still be together ...

I looked down at my Finn.

He'd fallen asleep.

I thought, *Maybe he'll forget what I've just told him.*

But he remembered.

Two days later, I picked him up from nursery.

"'Lo, Mummy," he said. "Where's Dan?"

When Daniel rang to tell me Finn was safe and sound, I burst into tears of joy.

The story made headlines in the local papers the next day and Daniel told me the Davenports had the press hanging around outside the house, begging for more details. He said Jade was great – really strong and confident now that she'd admitted to being Finn's mum. She told reporters she had nothing more to say, and eventually they drifted away, with their grubby notebooks and their cameras, to suck at someone else's life . . .

He said, "I'm so glad I can be here for her, Laura," and I could hear the pride in his voice. "She's my rainbow girl."

Two days later, they arrived on my doorstep unexpectedly.

The boy, with Jade. He was carrying a basket. I couldn't believe it. A Labrador puppy with a soft, squashy little face and eyes to melt your heart.

"This is Oscar," Daniel said. "We rescued him from the Blue Cross sanctuary . . . Jade and I, we wanted to say thank you – you know, for helping with Finn."

I was completely overwhelmed. Nobody's ever said thank you like that to me before.

Oscar started scampering all over the cottage. Muffin took one look at him and shot out of the window. The beginning of another wonderful relationship . . .

I gave them tea and we talked. Daniel starts school again soon. Jade's planning to study singing. I felt it was the end of the summer – and yet I had a sense that everything, like Oscar and me, was just starting to happen.

And so I found myself telling them.

You know.

About *her*.

I'd been eighteen, just about to go to Somerville.

I met a postgraduate called Graham. We started an affair. I liked him but I wasn't besotted, I wasn't madly in love. I couldn't believe it when I realised I was going to have a baby.

Daddy said, "You'll have to take a year off, Laura. Go down to Cornwall and have the child there. Get it adopted."

So I did.

That was thirty-seven years ago. And yet it feels like yesterday.

I told Daniel and Jade that in those days, things were different. Nobody talked about sex. Daddy and I could never have looked after a baby, not in the way Jade had done with her parents.

I told her I thought she was wonderful, the way she and her mum and dad had coped, the way she'd admitted everything to help with the appeal.

I told them I'd decided: I was going to try to trace my daughter. God, it felt incredible to call her that.

My daughter.

As soon as I've finished Daddy's book, I'm going to camp out at the Public Records Office in London. Trace the birth certificate. Then trace the records of her adoption.

Daddy and I had called her Maria. On the certificate. It had been my mother's name.

But I didn't know what her new family called her.

And I wanted to know so much . . .

There was a crash of plates in the kitchen. Oscar had begun to find his feet.

I bustled in to clear it all up. I could hear Daniel and Jade whispering together. When I came back, Jade's face was flushed. She gave me a hug and said it was Finn's birthday on Saturday and would I like to come to his party?

"It's a forget-the-future party," Daniel added — and a look passed between him and Jade that I couldn't fathom. There was love in it, but also something dark and secret and somehow full of pain.

Something he hasn't told me and maybe never will.

"Bring Oscar," Jade said quickly, and the puppy jumped happily on to her lap. "Finn will adore him. It'll be mayhem and wonderful."

I said wild horses wouldn't keep me away.

I held Oscar in my arms. He was light and warm. He started to lick my face.

My new Barnaby.

And I waved to Jade and Daniel from the door as they walked off, hand in hand.

They timed it very carefully, so everyone knew exactly where they should be.

Laura's car drew up outside Jade's door.

Daniel said, "Jade." He kissed her lips. "Laura's just arrived."

Jade said, "Finn, quick, let's go and tell Granny Eve that Laura's here."

She scuttled Finn away.

Eve darted into the living-room.

Daniel opened the door.

Oscar leaped into the hall and bounded into the kitchen.

Finn squealed with delight.

"Hi," Laura said. "These presents are for Finn . . . You look very smart."

He hugged her. "Specially for you," he said. "Come and meet everyone."

They moved into the living-room.

"Clare . . . Martin . . . Bobby . . . Eve . . . I'd like you to meet Laura."

She shook everyone's hand.

Daniel looked into Laura's eyes: a speckled grey, bright, attentive, like a bird's.

They smiled at each other.

"Laura —" he swallowed back the tears — "Laura's my new gran."

"I am, aren't I?" They stood with their arms around each other. "I really am."

Coming of Age

When her mother is killed in a riding accident, nine-year-old Amy is mute and traumatised. She cannot remember what happened and she is haunted by a nightmare she cannot fully explain. She becomes obsessed with her father, clinging for dear life to their relationship.

Six years later, the chance discovery of a postcard gives her the clue she needs to uncover the truth about the past. It takes her to Italy, to a man she has never met. Was he her mother's lover – or her killer?

The threads of the past lead inexorably back to the present and, as they gradually allow her to remember those horrific moments she thought forever buried, finally - and in more ways than one - Amy comes of age.

ISBN 0 689 83772 0

Girl in the Attic

Thirteen-year-old Nathan is furious when Mum hauls him off to Cornwall for Christmas and then tells him they are to move there for good.

He wants to be back with Dad, with his best friend, Tom, with his London life.

But then he finds a cottage and a girl. The girl in the attic.

Who is she, and what is the family secret that haunts her life?

Valerie Mendes' gripping, fast-moving novel explores the whirlpools of change in teenagers' lives, the strengths of friendship, and the inescapable, binding pull of love.

ISBN 0 689 83680 5